California
Journey

A TRUE LOVE STORY

ERNA M. HOLYER

REVIEW AND HERALD® PUBLISHING ASSOCIATION
HAGERSTOWN, MD 21740

Copyright © 1997 by
Review and Herald® Publishing Association
International copyright secured

The author assumes full responsibility for the accuracy of
all facts and quotations as cited in this book.

This book was
Edited by Jeannette R. Johnson
Designed by DeLaine Heinlein-Mayden
Interior illustrations by Mary Bausman
Cover art by Joel Spector
Typeset: 12/13 Optima

PRINTED IN U.S.A.

01 00 99 98 97   5 4 3 2 1

R&H Cataloging Service
Holyer, Erna Marie, 1925-
    California journey.

    Series: Vienna Brooks Saga.

    I. Title.   II. Series: Vienna Brooks Saga.

        813.54

ISBN 0-8280-0963-5

Dedication

*To two fine teachers who helped shape my life . . .
Norma R. Youngberg, my first writing teacher, and
Clyde Arbuckle, teacher of Western history.*

Contents

Introduction

In preparing a term paper for a history class, I discovered C. B. Glasscock's, *A Golden Highway*. This book mentioned a 12-year-old boy, Elisha Brooks, who delivered milk to gold miners in Bidwell Bar, California, in 1853, picked up a dollar's worth of gold dust in wagon ruts after a rain, and bought an orange from Tahiti. He planted the seeds and grew the first orange tree in Butte County, California.

Intrigued, I asked historians and librarians for research clues. *A Pioneer Mother of California,* a slim volume written by Elisha Brooks, turned up at Bancroft Library, University of California at Berkeley. It dealt with the westward trek of a mother and her six young children. The story moved me deeply.

Columnists of the San Jose *Mercury News* helped me locate people who remembered Elisha Brooks. A grandson, Edmund Worth Whitney, granted me an interview and gave me further leads. Another grandson, Brooks Scholfield Whitney, invited me to a cottage in the Pacific Coast Range, where Elisha spent his retirement years. He showed me Elisha's workshop. I saw a magnificent redwood burl tabletop his grandfather had made, Elisha's wing chair, and the mossy apple orchard in which Elisha's ashes were scattered.

Learning about my intention to write about his family,

Mr. Whitney entrusted me with a box filled with handwritten reminiscences and speeches, diary pages, and scrapbooks containing newspaper clippings and family news. Elisha had saved certificates, correspondence, poems, sketches and photos. An album, Elisha's 1894 Christmas present for his wife, Nellie, yielded a wealth of information. The *San Francisco Public School Record, Pacific School and Home Journal,* and *Girls High School Journal* carried biographical sketches of Elisha. Another album, labeled *"Mrs. Elisha Brooks,"* dated June 10, 1904, was devoted to the Worth family.

In sorting and evaluating the material, I also found J. H. Zumwalt's letter of August 1, 1860, describing Vienna's death; Elisha's Life Diploma (teaching credential), dated September 24, 1878, and his obituary that read: *His entire boyhood was a struggle for education.*

Correspondence with John H. Nopel, president of the Butte County Historical Society and editor of the society's quarterly publication, *Diggins,* gave proof that Elisha's mother had taught at Bidwell Bar in 1853, and that his father was a Butte County resident during the 1850 Census. Articles in *Diggins* shed further light on people and happenings.

Trips to Berry Creek, Oroville, and Bidwell Bar gave me a feel for these locations. I remember wandering along the gravel banks of the Feather River (where the twins delivered milk to gold miners), and marveling at the old suspension bridge in its original location before the area was flooded and became known as Lake Oroville.

A visit to the Wells Fargo history center in San Francisco turned up an 1898 photo of 26 identified pupils at Girls' High School, making me realize that the 1906 earthquake had obliterated much of this city's history.

Letters from Isabelle Brooks De Rosa, a granddaughter who lived with Elisha and Nellie during her school years, as well as letters from Teresa Hess and Gladys D. Hoagland shed light on Elisha's character and provided insight into the family life and circumstances of Elisha and Nellie Brooks. Memories related by Alice Wilder showed the great regard in which Elisha Brooks was held at Ben Lomond. History centers of several libraries furnished the needed background information.

Elisha had safeguarded the memories of people and events that would otherwise be lost. His notes perpetuated the memory of his pioneer mother; his sister, Vienna, and the circumstances of her love, marriage, and untimely death; his oxen, Nig and Brock, and the young teamsters; the grueling westward trek; the emigrants' start in the gold country; and his struggle to become a teacher.

The Brooks family spun a web around me. Increasingly, I felt that God was urging me to write their story for today's readers. It's been 30 years since I first learned about that 12-year-old boy. Years of detective work finally yielded the necessary documentation. I am grateful for the opportunity to see this story through and hope that the published books in the Vienna Brooks Saga, *A Wilderness Journey, Golden Journey,* and *California Journey,* will give readers a truly moving and uplifting experience.

I wish to thank everybody, named or unnamed, who made these books possible. God bless you!

Erna M. Holyer
San Jose, California

Vienna's brother, Elisha Brooks

Chapter One
Farewell

Elisha Brooks took a shortcut to his parents' cottage near Bidwell Bar, California. Joy crept into his weary bones. Behind him lay the rumbling sawmill with its hazy wood smoke. He whistled a silly tune he had learned from the lumbermen. Dry branches snapped underfoot and cones crackled in the pine duff. He entered a canyon and hurried downhill beside a babbling brook.

The garden came into view, then the cottage. Two small blond boys played in the autumn sunshine beneath the fluttering wash out front.

"Jay! Joseph!" he called.

The boys looked up with puzzled expressions. *They don't remember me!* Elisha thought in dismay.

Two bigger boys entered the yard, lugging wooden buckets from the spring. When they saw Elisha, they set down the pails so fast that water splashed out. "Elisha! It's our brother!" they cried. The boys ran toward the teenager, who caught them in his arms.

"Where's Justus?" Elisha demanded, missing the family's middle child.

"Working at a sawmill." Orion's clear blue eyes showed excitement.

"Since when?"

"Since last spring. Pa sent me then, too. He said I was 12 years old and big enough for sawmill work."

"What happened, Orion?"

"The lumber boss told me to 'put some meat on them bones and come back next year.' "

"Will you try again?" Elisha wanted to know.

"Yes, I will!" Orion pointed to his younger brother. "Pa wants Elmont to come with me. He says we both can earn money."

Elisha frowned. Ten-year-old Elmont hadn't grown much. The boy had survived without milk on the westward journey in 1852 and after coming to California. Orion also looked small for his age. Elisha felt sorry for his brothers. "You're too young for the hard work at a sawmill," he said.

"No, we're not," Orion insisted. "Pa worked at the woolen mill back East when he was our age. He helped support his family."

"I know, Orion, but what does Mother say?"

The door of the little cottage opened and a tall, slim woman stepped over the threshold.

"Elisha, son!"

Elisha spun around. "Mother!" He flew into her arms. As she hugged him tenderly, long-forgotten feelings of warmth and security overwhelmed Elisha. He felt like the youngster he once had been in the backwoods of St. Joseph County, Michigan.

She released him. "Let me look at you, son! What a splendid young man you are!" Joy over seeing him colored her cheeks. She fetched the two little boys, 4-year-old Jay and 2-year-old Joseph. Leading them by the hand, she brought them to Elisha. "This is your big brother, children. Give him a big kiss."

Elisha lifted the boys and whirled them around. Jay

squealed like a happy piglet, but Joseph kicked and cried. Elisha handed him back to Mother. She bounced the toddler in her arms and pointed to the garden. "We planted new roses," she said proudly. "What lovely flowers and scents! The grapevines produced their first clusters." She laughed. "A mother raccoon helped herself to the crop. The two orange trees you grew from seeds are growing, and we have beets, turnips, carrots, onions, and pumpkins. What good taste! We're enjoying our kitchen garden, thanks to you and Elijah. You boys broke the sod in this virgin soil." She stopped herself. "What brings you home, son?"

Elisha grinned mischievously. "I smelled your biscuits and my taste buds acted up," he teased.

She looked puzzled. "What else?"

"I want to attend school, Mother. I'm finding out that I don't know much. Men from the States can figure things out because they know. They say they learned useful things at school."

Elisha weakened under his mother's gaze, and heat crept over his face. The truth was that the lumbermen had made cutting remarks. Their unfeeling laughter when he answered their tricky questions still hurt. He decided to swallow his pride and tell her the truth. "The boss man said he'd promote me, Mother. He gave me a test. He said every man who got promoted had to take this test." Elisha lifted his eyes to hers. "I couldn't read the questions, Mother. I could have done the job, for I watched how grown men do it, but I couldn't pass that silly test."

"What did your boss say?"

"He said"—Elisha swallowed the lump in his throat— "'You're a good worker, Brooks. However, I haven't any use for a stupid head like yours. You'll strip bark for the rest of your life.'"

Mother patted his hand. "We shall talk with your father." She drew him to the lean-to filled with wood shavings and carpenter's tools.

Father was astride a sawhorse, planing a piece of wood. His steel-gray eyes widened as Elisha explained that he wanted to enter grammar school. "Give up a paying job? Sit in grammar school at age 17? Who will support the family?" he challenged.

Elisha unrolled the handful of dollars in his handkerchief. He handed over a year's worth of hard earned wages. "This will keep you in food for a while, Pa."

Mother protested. "What about you, Elisha? How will you keep yourself in food?"

"I can do odd jobs, Mother—drive a team, or chop wood."

"Where is this school?" Father wanted to know.

"In Oroville, Pa. I heard of its opening while delivering milk more than a year ago." Elisha didn't dare add "before our farm went bankrupt."

Father frowned.

"The school is nothing fancy like the academy Vienna attended, Pa. The Oroville school teaches the three R's." Sweat beads rolled down Elisha's brow. He spoke quickly for fear of losing courage.

Mother came to his aid. "With Elijah and Justus working, we can survive without Elisha's wages, dearest." She smiled brightly. "You know how well Vienna did at the academy. Our daughter graduated as valedictorian. She made us proud."

Father grunted, but his eyes shone. "Our daughter could have done better than marry into a dry goods store," he muttered. "A pretty girl like that could have married—"

Mother cut him off. "She loves John, dearest."

Father sighed. "I miss that girl around the house."

"Vienna is happy," Mother asserted. "We now must think of Elisha's future."

"He has a future at the sawmill," Father said.

Mother shook her head. "What future is there for a boy who cannot read? Our son has forgotten what little he learned back in Michigan. Why, he attended school only three winters. He was 9 when he helped me with farm work after you left for the gold mines. Then he drove the covered wagon to California, worked for a miner, delivered milk in the mining camps, and labored at the sawmill." Mother stood tall. "Elisha has done right by us, dearest. We must not stand in his way. This is 1858, and he's 17 years old."

Father pulled himself up on the homemade crutches he'd been using for the past five years to steady himself. He had never regained the health he'd lost years before as a result of malaria he'd contracted from the swamps of Michigan. "So it is; our son will attend school." Turning to Elisha, he said, "Learn something and make us proud, son. Now what's to eat? I'm hungry."

After a meal of warm biscuits and mixed vegetables, Mother and his brothers accompanied Elisha outside. "You mustn't mind your father's mood," Mother told Elisha. "Your father is in pain."

Elisha nodded. "I know." To get her mind off Father he asked about Vienna. "Has my sister written any letters, Mother? How is she? Do you know?"

Mother's face lit up. "She is happy, son. She's learning all there is to learn about John's mercantile business, and she cares for John's mother, Mrs. Zumwalt, when she suffers from her sick headaches."

Elisha hoisted his bedroll. "A year has passed since Vienna's wedding, Mother. It makes me sad to think I missed her big day."

A worry line crowded Mother's high forehead. "I'm sorry we couldn't send word to you in time, son." Then she brightened. "Vienna had a wonderful wedding right here in the garden. You ought to have have seen her! She was a beautiful bride."

"Did she miss me?" he asked.

"Oh, yes! She missed especially you, Elisha. I believe she wanted to tell you something important."

"She did?" Elisha felt warm. "Is there a baby yet?"

"No, son."

He shot a quick glance at his mother. Fine lines showed in her oval face. Was she worried about Vienna? Was anything wrong? He set down his bedroll and put his arms around her. "Let me do something special for you, Mother. Do you have a wish I can fulfill?"

"You are so good to me, son." She held his embrace. Her large, clear eyes rested on his face. The steady, penetrating gaze seemed to fathom the pit of his soul. "Son."

She said it softly, and he sensed that she wanted to say more. But the fine curves of her mouth trembled in an uncertain smile, and the words remained unsaid. Not wanting to press her, he traced her cheeks with his fingers. How beautiful she was and how precious! He wanted to always remember her like this, with her smooth brown hair combed into thick braids resting on the crisp, white collar of her dress.

He broke away. "I'll be back at the end of the school year, Mother," he promised and shouldered his bundle and marched off.

"Brother, wait!" Elmont ran after him. "Take me with you, brother!"

Elisha stooped and hugged the boy. "Stay here, Elmont. Mother needs you to look after her."

The boy's lips trembled, but he turned back to the cottage. Elisha was just turning onto the path leading to Butte County's "City of Gold" when heart-stopping screams made him turn around. Mother was holding up little Jay, who stretched out both arms toward him.

"Farewell, son! God bless you!" Mother called.

A sob caught in Elisha's throat, and his feet turned to leave.

Chapter Two
City of Gold

A passerby might have wondered at the comings and goings at a miner's cabin in Oroville, Butte County's "City of Gold." However, people didn't venture outdoors much during those damp, dark winter days. Many nursed a sick friend or family member. Many buried a loved one. The winter rains had set in early in 1858, the year Elisha enrolled in grammar school. Typhoid fever attacked people living in the gulches and canyons of the gold country, and spread with terrifying speed.

Inside the miner's cabin, Elisha lay gravely ill. Wracked by fever, he drifted in and out of consciousness for two days. Then a rush of air entered the cabin along with the teacher. The school man had missed his big student. Fearing the worst, he had searched the small town until he found Elisha in the unheated cabin. He built a fire, then straddled the stool beside the boy's crude bunk. Rain prattled against the roof and the wind howled.

The patient tossed and turned, babbling incoherently.

"Brooks! Can you hear me, Brooks?" The teacher smoothed the crumpled blanket over the delirious youth and waited.

In his delirium, Elisha fought against a childhood night-

mare. He was gazing out the window of a neighbor's log cabin. A black cloud rose on the horizon and spiraled over the heavens, turning day into inky night. Lightning scared him. Thunder made him wince. The fireworks were followed by a sighing breeze that changed first into a moan, then into a wind that shrieked like the wildest demons. Every movable thing began to play leapfrog. Fence rails, chicken coops, and haystacks turned somersaults, flew over the house, and went sailing through the air. The barn roof spread like wings and headed for a distant swamp.

Father fastened the window shutters outside. A neighbor hastened down to his cellar. Elisha ran behind him, skidding to a halt as the man clapped the trapdoor shut. Then Father hurried inside and slammed the door. A rush of wind hurled the door open again, and Elisha tumbled in and fell against the wall. During a lull in the storm, Father fetched a heavy pole and used it to bolt the door shut. Elisha lay on the floor, covering his ears, hoping to shut out the infernal noises.

"Brooks! Brooks!" The schoolmaster shook the whimpering youth.

But Elisha dreamed on.

"We'd best go home," his father said.

So they left the neighbor's house and saw that the hurricane had mowed a swath through the forest like a reaper through a wheat field. Trees blocked the road. It took all of Elisha's strength to climb over them.

At home, the barn had collapsed and its timbers lay scattered. The windows and the shake roof of the cabin were missing. Wheat sheaves had flown away. Father broke into a run.

"Don't leave me, Pa!" Elisha screamed.

The schoolmaster filled a cup with water and held it to the boy's lips. "I shall summon help, Brooks."

"Where am I?" Elisha whispered.

"In your bed, Brooks. You are safe."

"Why am I in bed?" Elisha's teeth chattered. He tried to

sit up and focus his eyes. *Who was the man beside his bed?* he wondered.

Then the schoolmaster left and somebody else came in. Another dream tormented Elisha.

Little fellows in knee britches stood beside his bench at school, outreading him right and left. They giggled at Elisha's stuttering attempt to read a passage from the First Reader. A buggy stopped at the schoolhouse after school and a man looked for his son. Elisha ran toward the man, but he brushed Elisha off.

McGuffey's Third Reader was no mystery to the 10-year-old who jumped into his father's arms. "My dad reads with me at home," the youngster boasted. He climbed onto the buggy and stuck out his tongue.

Elisha moaned. Was it only yesterday the boy had read from McGuffey? Or was it a week ago? He recalled sentences the 10-year-old had rattled off with ease. Elisha's lips moved as he recited from McGuffey.

James Brown was 10 years old when his parents sent him to school. It was not far from home, and therefore they sent him by himself. But instead of going to school, he was in the habit of playing truant. He would go into the fields, or spend his time with idle boys. This was not all. He would falsely tell his mother that he had been to school, and had said his lessons very well.

"I did go to school, Mother!" Elisha whimpered. "I'm not playing truant."

A damp cloth cooled his hot forehead. Somebody was pouring smelly tea down his throat. Elisha woke up. "Not senna tea!" he protested, "I hate senna tea!"

Nodding off again, he saw his mother in a pine box. Her brown hair was carefully combed. Her chin and nose jutted from sunken cheeks. And in the background, a baby cried. Darkness smothered Elisha as strangers closed the lid of the pine box.

"Mother! Don't leave me alone, Mother!" he screamed.

"You're not alone, dear Elisha. I am with you." An angel's hand smoothed his brow.

Elisha felt alarm. Was he dying? Was he dead? He beat at the fair creature at his bedside. "Are you the boatman who's going to ferry me across?" he babbled.

The angel's laugh sounded like tinkling bells. "No, indeed! I brought you warm bread from my mother's oven." She lifted the white linen cloth from the basket beside his bunk.

Elisha felt cold, but he wasn't shaking.

A gentleman stepped into the firelight, taking the angel's place. "Are you feeling better, Brooks?"

Elisha recognized the doctor. "Have you been treating me?"

"Indeed, I have," the doctor chuckled.

Elisha reached under his mattress. "I owe you money. How much is my bill?"

The doctor whistled softly through his beard. "How much money do you have?"

"Two dollars."

"Put down all you have, and I'll do the same," the doctor ordered. "The one who has the least shall take the pile."

Elisha put down the two dollars he had earned doing odd jobs and driving a team of horses. It was all he owned, and his cupboards were empty.

The doctor put down three dollars. Eyes swimming, he pushed the money toward Elisha and hurried off with the girl Elisha had mistaken for an angel.

"Wait!" Elisha slid his wobbly legs over the bunk. His knees buckled and his head fell back. "I must ask the schoolmaster to return the doctor's money."

He itched. Lifting his shirt, he saw pink spots on his chest and abdomen. "Better not scratch too much," he muttered.

The aroma of freshly baked bread rising from the girl's basket made him hungry. He was munching crusty bread when the door opened and his twin brother walked into the cabin. Elijah dropped his bundle by the fire and peeled off his jacket. "Let me have a bite, brother. I've traveled a long way to see you."

Elisha thanked God for company. "Did the schoolmaster send for you?" he asked.

"No, Pa told me to find you."

"Why?"

Elijah broke off a piece of bread. "To tell you that Mother came down with the fever."

Elisha's heart missed a beat. "In a dream I saw Mother in a pine box . . . Is she . . ."

Elijah nodded sadly. "We buried her in the garden. She loved her roses."

A sob caught in Elisha's throat. *Mother dead?* He couldn't bear the thought. "I missed her funeral!" he sobbed.

Elijah grasped his hand. "She wouldn't want us to grieve. She always said, 'In God's scheme of things everything works out for the best.' Remember?"

Firelight flickered fitfully in the cabin's gloom. The brothers wept together. Mother had stood for everything good and gentle the twins had known. Elisha knew he'd sing her praises as long as he lived.

"What will happen to our brothers?" Elisha asked after a long pause.

Elijah blew his nose. "Settlers from the States took the boys. Jay, Joseph, Orion, and Elmont all live with different families."

"Elmont is afraid of strange men," Elisha worried aloud. "Let's hope he'll get used to strangers. We must help support Father and our brothers," Elisha suggested.

Elijah frowned. "It won't be easy, not with you sick, and me enrolling in grammar school."

"We must try," Elisha insisted.

A week later he opened the door to a gentleman in broadcloth suit and silk hat. "I am looking for Elisha Brooks," the man explained.

"That's me, sir." Elisha grasped the door to keep from wobbling.

"I should like to engage your services," the man proposed. "You were recommended to me by the schoolmaster."

"W-what can I do for you, sir?"

"I have a milk cow that is inclined to stray. I urgently need somebody to herd and milk this cow. I understand you are an expert at handling cows."

"I can do the milking and herding." Elisha wished he didn't feel so weak.

The gentleman hesitated. "There is one condition, though. You are required to live with my family."

"I can do that."

"Can you start tomorrow?"

"I can!" Elisha nodded with vigor.

The gentleman left his address, then lifted his hat in parting.

Before Elisha moved to the stranger's house, he asked his twin, "What does Mother expect from us, Elijah? What would she want us to do?"

"First of all, let's send word to Vienna," Elijah urged.

"I'll ask the schoolmaster to write the letter," Elisha said.

Elijah nodded. "Remember how proud Mother looked the day Vienna left for academy? She hoped our sister would become a teacher."

Elisha stared into the firelight. Odors of the hated senna tea were fading now that Elijah was brewing his healing herbs. "Vienna never wanted to teach, Elijah."

"I know. It was a big disappointment for Mother." He stared into the fire.

Elisha gave himself a push. "We must make up for Vienna."

"You and me—teachers? It would take a miracle to make teachers out of *us*," Elijah joked. But he wasn't laughing.

"Mother always said, 'By God's grace, all things are possible.'" Elijah put another log onto the fire, looking thoughtful.

Chapter Three
Grammar School

The spring sun took Elisha by surprise. Winter rains stopped and wildflowers burst into bloom. The blossoms turned happy faces toward the blue sky, splashing a rainbow of color across the countryside. Oaks and sycamores clothed with fresh new leaves resounded with the flutter and twitter of birds. Woodpeckers flew into holes high up on tree trunks, carrying food to noisy hatchlings.

Elisha gathered wildflowers from the hillsides and at the forest's edge to sell after school hours. Lupines, buttercups, lilies, irises, Indian pinks, blue-eyed grass, and fairy lanterns provided exciting bouquets that he tied together with tough grasses. To make his flower bunches extra attractive, he added tall ferns.

Thanks to the mysterious gentleman, Elisha recovered his strength after the typhoid fever. In his benefactor's home he slept in a real bed with downy pillows. He ate nutritious meals and enjoyed plenty of rest because the cow he was supposed to herd never strayed. After asking around, Elisha learned that the gentleman and his schoolmaster were brothers. Another brother, Anson Burlingame, was a member of the House of Representatives (and would later become the United States Minister to China).

As Elisha tied yellow violets together, he remembered that the six-month school term at Oroville was nearing its end. He and Elijah planned to work in the mountains during the summer to help support their father and younger brothers. With arms filled with flowers, he headed for Oroville.

The city was a busy place. Dogs barked, mules brayed, horses whinnied. Stagecoaches and express wagons clattered through the streets. Hoofbeats rang out and drivers shouted commands. Miners flocked into the town on horseback and muleback. The clamor was deafening.

Elisha dodged the swinging baskets of vegetables a pig-tailed Chinese man carried on a pole draped over husky shoulders. Somehow, he knew, this man eked out a living in this alien place. Frugal by nature the Chinese emigrants made a go of it, just like he and his brother would. He smiled at the man who lived among Chinatown's exotic odors and tinkling bells.

At the first hotel, Elisha peeked into a window. The bar room, draped in crimson calico, reflected decanters, jars of brandied fruit, and flowers in vases in its mirrors. Bluebells nodded in airy clusters. Lilies rose on haughty stems. Funnel-shaped blossoms marched up stately stalks. He had sold the flowers the day before, yet they still appeared fresh.

At the gambling saloon next door, men sat around tables wearing hats, chewing tobacco, and drinking liquor. Miners and gamblers in city clothes played games of cards at green-topped tables.

"Waste of money," Elisha muttered. "Whoever heard of a miner winning?"

Peeking upstairs at the next hotel, he glimpsed red curtains, a large sofa, and a table with wilting flowers. He scooted to the side entrance leading to the hotel's store and shop. Sights and smells of leather, flannel, velveteen, calico, and preserved meats tickled his imagination.

24

"Do you need fresh flowers?" he asked the lanky fellow behind the counter.

The man appraised Elisha's wares with a calculating eye. "Leave the violets and two large bunches." He counted out a few small coins.

Elisha left the violets with regret. He wished he could put them on his mother's grave. Mother had loved violets.

In a thoroughfare called Miner's Alley, he sold flowers in shops tucked away in brick buildings. He crossed the street at the corner restaurant. Wooden posts below the second story balcony of the popular St. Nicholas Hotel cast long shadows in the setting sun. Mules pricked up their long ears and horses nickered at hitching posts. Elisha scaled the foot-high wooden sidewalk, wondering what the ruckus was about inside. He peeked through the window.

A miner stood on a raised platform under the chandelier, squeezing into his concertina with all his might as strange "couples" did a shuffling dance to his music. For lack of women, the men were dancing with other men. Each "lady" dancer sported a red handkerchief around one arm. The men swung their "ladies" with as much fervor as the moving mass of dancers in the barroom allowed. Elisha laughed out loud. The sight of miners in slouch hats, flannel shirts, suspenders, and baggy pants tucked into top boots stepping on each others' toes was too funny for words.

Suddenly Elijah popped up beside him. "I've finished chopping wood," he reported. The twin pressed his nose against the window pane. "What are they doing?"

"Celebrating, I guess," Elisha answered.

"But it's not even dark yet."

"Makes no difference to them." Elisha moved to another window to get a better view. "Miners celebrate anytime; that's why saloons stay open around the clock."

"I once saw a miner who had the jim-jams," Elijah said. "He lay on the floor, shrieking and acting crazy. People said he had California fever, but the doctor called it *delir-*

ium tremens, and said the disease is caused by drinking too much alcohol."

"Drunkards go crazy around here," Elisha scoffed. "I guess that's why people call this town the devil's nest of California. They're proud of Oroville's 100 or more saloons and gambling places."

Just then the saloon door swung open. Two red-eyed miners staggered outside, their bloodshot gaze drilling into the boys.

"Let's go," Elisha said quietly.

The bigger fellow singled out Elijah. "Wanna go inside? I'm buying! Come, let's have some fun."

Elijah's fearful expression gave Elisha courage. "Leave my brother be!" he ordered. "He's running an errand and has no time to sit around."

Elijah sprinted away, leaving the miner staring in puzzled wonder. "Well, I'll be! He was just standing over yonder."

"You ain't seein' double," his partner sneered. "Them boys is twins."

The big fellow turned his attention to Elisha. "Come on, I'm buying," he said, gripping Elisha's arm and dragging him inside, past sweaty dancers.

"Leave me be! I don't drink whiskey," Elisha protested.

"Drink, I tell you!" the miner ordered.

"No whiskey for me!" Elisha insisted.

"Drink, or else!" the miner threatened.

"No whiskey for me!" Elisha repeated. "My angel mother always said any fool can empty a bottle, but it takes brains and discipline to resist a fool's teasing." His flowers slipped from his arm, and he stooped to retrieve them. Too late—they lay crushed beneath a dancer's boots.

The miner uttered unsavory words and poured the cold drink down the boy's collar. Elisha's yell drew a crowd of hilarious onlookers. Everybody quit dancing to enjoy the side show.

"His angel mother," they teased.

Stung by their laughter, Elisha elbowed his way outside.

At the end of the school year, Elisha packed his books. Mr. Burlingame, his wonderful schoolmaster, had awakened in him a love of learning and reading. By studying evenings, Elisha had managed to catch up with youngsters in pinafores who had outspelled him at first. The twins wrapped their books and other belongings into bundles and headed for the mountains.

They spent the summer transporting wagonloads of goods over the Sierra Nevada. As he sat on the jolting wagon, Elisha repeated syllables he'd learned from the McGuffey reader: "Vi-o-lent, fright-ful-ly, sis-ter . . ." Next fall he'd get ahead of his schoolmates and no longer be a laughingstock, Elisha promised himself.

That fall the twins descended the mountains and marched into Oroville with their younger brother, Elmont. Though he was 11, he looked no older than 8, because his growth had been stunted. He desperately missed his mother and had always distrusted men. He never had taken to Father. (Even while crossing the Plains in the covered wagon six years before, Elmont had kicked and screamed whenever a stranger picked him up.)

The three brothers moved into a large cabin that had been vacated by a miner. They all enrolled in school, then began to fix up the rundown place. Mr. Burlingame, their schoolmaster and a man of gentlemanly deportment, surprised the boys when he asked if he could share their cabin. The learned and warm-hearted man soon became the boys' role model.

"You are doing exceptionally well in your studies," Mr. Burlingame informed the twins. "If you desire to advance beyond the grammar school level, I should be delighted to help you further in your studies."

So the twins added botany, astronomy, and physics to their regular studies and progressed steadily with Mr. Burlingame's help.

One evening after Elmont had cleared the table and plunged the tin dishes into the pan for scrubbing, Mr. Burlingame said he had an announcement. The boys looked at their teacher expectantly.

"My revelation tonight may surprise you, dear friends," Mr. Burlingame began. "I have been chosen as the incoming president of Healdsburg Academy, a fine educational institution in Sonoma County."

Elisha gulped. "Does this mean you won't teach here anymore?"

A smile brightened the schoolmaster's pleasant features. "Yes, I shall leave Oroville at the end of the term. Would you like to know more about Healdsburg?"

"Yes, sir." Elisha was almost dizzy with thoughts crashing around in his head. Lose his wonderful teacher? He couldn't bear the thought.

"Healdsburg is situated near the Russian River, among beautiful hills and an eminence called Fitch Mountain," Mr. Burlingame began. "An emigrant from Missouri, Mr. Harmon Heald, built a cabin and store near the main road. Mr. Heald obtained 100 acres at auction from Señora Josefa Carrillo, widow of Captain Henry Delano Fitch, an American shipmaster, who owned the huge Rancho Sotoyome land grant.

"Other American pioneers joined Mr. Heald and expressed a desire to educate their children at an advanced Christian school," Mr. Burlingame continued. "A town site was surveyed in 1857, and God-fearing settlers donated money for a school and three churches." Mr. Burlingame rubbed his hands, smiling.

"The academy has attracted scholars, an adequate number of students, and instruction commenced last year, about the time you first enrolled in grammar school, Elisha." He hesitated. "Should you boys decide to attend Healdsburg Academy you will need funds for tuition, room, and board."

Silence followed the schoolmaster's disclosure. Elisha spoke at last. "We will miss you, sir. We have no money."

Mr. Burlingame contemplated the twins for a long moment. "I shall recommend you for scholarships. Free tuition is granted to poor but outstanding students."

Elisha eyebrows shot up. "Accepting something for nothing isn't right."

The schoolmaster looked pensive. "Do not rush your decision, dear pupils. Discuss the situation among yourselves. Your future depends upon your state of education. Academy is a key that can open doors to future opportunities."

Elisha's innards lurched. The teacher knew all that was written in books and much that happened in real life. Ask him and he knew. "Accepting something for nothing isn't right," he repeated, hating himself for the disappointed look on his teacher's face.

"Let's think about it, brother," Elijah suggested.

Mr. Burlingame nodded. The subject wasn't mentioned again. Teacher and pupils studied by the light of a pitch pine knot until eyelids grew heavy.

The moon bathed the cabin in cool, white light. While the last log sputtered into the ashes, Elisha tossed in his bunk and thought of all he had learned. His eyes roamed from the iron kettle, Dutch oven, frying pan, table, and three-legged stools to the shelf filled with books. His heart swelled at the prospect of future learning. Healdsburg Academy sounded like paradise. How much money did travel, tuition, room, and board cost? He despaired until he remembered that he and Elijah had managed to put Vienna through academy. And now their sister was handling tasks required of her in John's merchandise establishment, thanks to the instruction she had received at the academy. Could he and Elijah, the wild boys whose minds had gone to weeds, accept Mr. Burlingame's high-flying advice?

The end of the school year arrived with terrifying speed. Between selling wildflowers and completing the grammar school course ahead of his schoolmates, Elisha labored over a speech the teacher had requested.

On the last day of school, Mr Burlingame announced that Elisha Brooks would give the farewell address. Elisha stepped up front and faced his fellow students, his knees trembling and his mouth dry.

Is this what it's like to be a teacher? he wondered. *Everybody looking at you, expecting words of wisdom?* The paper shook in his hands. He felt like running until he remembered Mr. Burlingame's advice to concentrate on the speech.

"Dear friends," Elisha began. "I stand before you for the last time, and it is with the deepest feelings of regret that I bid you farewell." He wiped his forehead. Chopping wood was easier than this.

"I have been with you a long time, pursuing knowledge. I have been a sharer in your joys and sorrows and have become attached—" He dabbed at his eyes and missed an entire paragraph.

"You cannot feel the pangs of parting as I do, for you can visit each other. Not so with me!" He glanced at Elmont and Elijah and ached at the thought of his scattered little brothers. "E're another week passes, I shall be far from here among the rugged mountains, where solitude reigns undisturbed, save for the occasional visits of the Red man and wild beasts, from where I can seldom, if ever come to see you.

"Yet I leave not all behind. My books shall be my companions. And in lonely evening hours they shall be my comforters and instructors.

"My friends," Elisha continued, "though I may never see you again, I shall think of you often. The remembrance of times spent in your company will make me long to get back. To know that I am not forgotten by you will be my joy."

He skipped entire paragraphs, including a poem he had carefully rhymed. His voice failed him until he noticed the teacher's encouraging nod.

"Dear schoolmates, if I have ever offended any of you, I ask your forgiveness. If any animosities exist between us, let us forget them and part friends.

"To our teacher, who has labored so faithfully to instill in our hearts the love of knowledge and language, I express my feelings of gratitude. His memory shall be cherished in my heart.

"And now, dear school, farewell! And oh, dear teacher, fellow students, playmates, farewell!" Elisha stepped down.

Mr. Burlingame's eyes swam as he thanked Elisha for his speech. Students rushed forward from their benches and threw their arms around him.

Elijah hugged him and said, "You'll make a wonderful teacher, brother. Let's do our utmost to get to Healdsburg. If God wants us to become teachers, He will help us."

Chapter Four
"Cowherd"

⟵⟶

This should do it." Elisha double-checked the cabin. He had packed his belongings, including wildflowers he had dried. Perhaps somebody somewhere could tell him their true names.

Elijah pointed to Elmont, who was wrapping a McGuffey's Reader and a clean shirt into his blanket. Any moment now Elmont would throw a tantrum. The tiny youngster had been doing the shopping, cooking, and cleaning. He never forgot to stoke the fire, wash the dishes, or make himself useful in a dozen different ways. Like a puppy, he was eager to please.

Elisha dreaded the thought of sending him back to foster parents. Mr. Burlingame had already checked out, and the twins' belongings were packed. Time to leave Oroville, the City of Gold.

"You know that we're leaving for Bidwell, don't you, Elmont?" Elisha broached the touchy subject.

Elmont tied his bundle. "I'm not coming with you."

"What do you mean, you're not coming with us?"

Elmont's face erupted in a rare smile. "Don't trouble yourself about me, Elisha. I'll stay here."

Elisha's mouth fell open. "Where?"

"At a dry goods store in Miner's Alley, the one that has the big G in the iron door."

Elisha's head spun. Elmont was a shrewd bargainer who could total up pennies in a flash. On days when Elmont helped sell wildflowers, the boy brought home cash. "A G in the door?" he asked, puzzled.

"It stands for *God* bless this house."

"Says who?"

"The proprietor's wife. You know her. She's big and friendly. She always gives good measure. She needs a boy like me to help with chores."

Elisha's memory clicked. The woman had bought flowers and never quibbled about the price. She was a motherly type, kind and easygoing.

Elmont's blue eyes sparkled. "She wants me, Elisha, she really does! She has a bunk for me, and she'll feed me."

Elisha hugged his brother. Choked with emotion, he said, "God bless the good woman."

Calypso, Fairy-Slipper
Calypso bulbosa

The twins accompanied Elmont to the dry goods store, where the big woman welcomed him with open arms. Relieved, the twins gathered up their picks and shovels and headed for the abandoned mining sites. Celestials had already worked over the deserted mines with Chinese thoroughness, yet the Brooks boys staked their hopes on finding enough "color" to finance the 250-mile journey to Healdsburg.

Gold mining demanded strength and endurance. Day after day, the twins stood in the cold water. The midday sun beat down and mosquitoes swarmed in maddening numbers. Golden specks in the pan looked miniscule compared to the mountains of dirt the twins shoveled.

The twins labored in the morning coolness and in the afternoon shade. Rather than toiling in the dizzying midday heat, they spent that time gathering wild greens for wholesome meals. Adhering to Mother's cooking methods, they spurned the miners' diet of dried and salted meats, believing it prepared the system for disease. When hunger gnawed, they added fish to their wild vegetables. Berries gleaned from the riverbank provided dessert. Tea brewed with Elijah's "yarbs" kept them in good health.

After six months of toil, the twins exchanged their "color" for $82. Would this grand sum get them to Healdsburg and back? They trusted in God and banked on their resourcefulness and thrift.

With money sewn into their belts and bundles thrown over their shoulders, they walked the 40 miles to Marysville, then took steerage passage to San Francisco. Stepping off the steamer's swaying plank, the young men shrugged into blankets they had thrown about themselves. The sharp wind blowing through the narrow Golden Gate strait stung. Shivering in the drifting fog, they watched the waterfront's hustle and bustle.

Stevedores rolled up barrels to a man standing on a horse drawn cart, who received the shipment. Celestials balanced jugs suspended from bamboo poles. Mexicans in sombreros and serapes jabbered beside a stack of boxes. Gentlemen in high-topped hats checked luggage coming off a ship.

Elisha's flesh crawled; he couldn't help it. People had described "Frisco" as a city of lurid crimes. Merchants and miners recounted stories of young men who were "shanghaied." Drugged or beaten senseless, these unfortunate victims were dragged aboard vessels needing hands, never to be seen or heard from again. He nearly fainted as a shady character popped out of the fog in front of him.

"Do you need a room for the night?" the man asked.

"We need a place to sleep," Elisha replied roughly.

"This way, gentlemen." The stranger led the way to the hulls of swaying ships.

"We can't pay much," Elisha explained.

"Follow me, please." The shifty-eyed character guided them to a ship and urged them up a rope ladder.

Elisha felt goose bumps. "Where is this ship going?" he asked, wishing his voice didn't crack.

"This isn't a seagoing ship," the guide informed him. "Businesses have existed on sailing ships ever since gold-seekers abandoned them. This way please."

For a modest fee, the hotel runner escorted the twins to a smelly, vermin-infested cubbyhole.

The moment the stranger was out of earshot, Elijah said, "This place is a trap, brother."

Elisha groped for a bunk, trying to stem his terror. About midnight he heard the sound of stealthy footsteps. Through the unlatched door he saw the outlines of two burly men. Knives flashed in the men's hands as they moved past.

"Give us your money and come along!" Rough voices grew loud in the adjoining cabin.

A shot rang out and the intruders fled, cursing and bumping into each other in their haste to get away.

The next morning the twins left that ramshackle hotel

and boarded the ferryboat bound for Petaluma. They thanked the Lord for their narrow escape from the wicked city by the Bay.

They walked the last 20 miles from Petaluma to Healdsburg Academy, where they enrolled. Politely refusing free tuition, they secured employment as janitors.

At the opening session, Mr. Burlingame, the academy's new president, welcomed the pupils. "As the school bell echoes through the streets, society will become more refined," Mr. Burlingame began. "Bright and smiling young people have arrived at this fine academy and, ere long, will listen to learned professors, as well as strengthen their knowledge, skills, and faith. Welcome to this working-man's college for young Christian men and women."

The former grammar school teacher and the professors he introduced wore black broadcloth suits, boiled white shirts, and elegant cravats. Trimmed beards, fancy mustaches, and groomed hair added to their unruffled perfection. A glance around the room revealed pupils who dressed as well as the professors. Elisha slicked back his hair, noticing for the first time his threadbare clothes and frayed sleeves.

After opening ceremonies, Mr. Burlingame greeted the twins. "So glad you could come!" he exclaimed. "I am well aware of your financial situation. If you wish, you may graduate with extra studies at the end of our six-month term. I shall speak to your professors." He beamed his warm smile. "Have you found a place to stay yet?"

Before Elisha could answer in the negative, his old schoolmaster was surrounded by professors and pupils. A hale and hearty fellow offered to share his cottage, if he could eat with the twins. Delighted, the twins accepted. As it turned out, the pudgy fellow had a ravenous appetite and moved out within a week "to get something to eat and save my life." Since he let the twins stay at his cottage, they voted him a good but misguided fellow.

Janitorial work put Elisha in poor stead with certain fellow students. Elegant youths turned up their noses at the classmate who cleaned halls and classrooms after school. One evening a student returned to the classroom to retrieve a pair of forgotten gloves.

"Who's by the teacher's desk?" he asked sharply.

Elisha, who was scrubbing the dais, straightened up.

"Why, Brooks, what are you doing here?" The youth's eyebrows went up in surprise. He was a tall and slender sprig, whose smirky smile annoyed Elisha.

"I work for my tuition," Elisha explained.

"You do? How quaint! Why doesn't your pater pay for it?"

"My pa—I mean, my father—is an invalid."

"A cripple?"

"He walks on crutches."

"What about your mother, doesn't she send you any money?"

"She, uh, cannot send any money." Elisha couldn't discuss his beloved mother with this unfeeling young man.

"What did you do at home?" The youth's sandy hair rose to a wavy tuft on top of his head. Limp strands hung down over a pair of flat ears, and his nose ended in a bulb that contrasted with his elegance and haughty bearing.

"I milked and herded my family's cows and sold the milk to gold miners." Elisha spoke with pride.

"You're a *cowherd?"* The youth's lips curled. "I'm glad you don't sit near me, Brooks, for you smell of barnyard." He slapped his white gloves against the desk and exited, laughing.

Elisha swallowed his anger. *I'm lucky to be here,* he told himself. *The academy is a wonderful place, and I'm allowed to study.* He liked the broad steps, tall windows, and clock tower that graced the two-story structure set against sloping hills. *It's an honor to keep this school clean, no matter what White Gloves says.*

Elisha made good use of his time. Rising at 4:00 a.m.,

he studied algebra, plane and solid geometry, trigonometry, two books of Harkness' Latin, Quackenbos' Philosophy, history, and English literature.

After reading a lesson, he fixed it in his mind. He mulled over lectures while going about menial tasks. In the classroom he recited his lessons with ease.

His professors spoke with modulated voices, expecting to be understood, and excelled at politeness, addressing Elisha as "Mr. Brooks." They demanded politeness and respect in return. Professors lectured without explaining in great detail. Pupils were expected to study their books in order to comprehend subjects and answer test questions.

Elisha was glad he had studied major subjects ahead of time. Thanks to Mr. Burlingame's generous help at the Oroville cabin, he found himself ahead of his class. He thought other students hated him for that, and that's why they called him "cowherd" and said his clothes smelled of barnyard. Because their parents had money and influence in the community, rich youths felt superior to poor boys. They equated their parents' worth with their own and felt no need to try hard.

Elijah chafed under his classmates' condescension. One evening he stormed out of the academy, leaving Elisha to finish the cleanup.

"What happened?" Elisha asked when he arrived at home.

His brother's eyelids looked red and swollen. "They made fun of me," Elijah complained. "They called me cowherd and said I smell. I'm leaving, Elisha!"

Through the window, Elisha saw White Gloves parading up and down in front of the cottage. "I wonder what charge he gets out of making us feel bad," he muttered.

"I can do without him and his friends, Elisha. Let's go home!"

"Let's not give up, Elijah. What would Mother say?" Elisha couldn't bear the thought.

The next morning a new girl entered Latin class. Standing gracefully by the teacher's desk, she explained that her parents had moved from San Francisco to Healdsburg so she could receive a Christian education.

The girl set Elisha's heart aflutter. As she introduced herself to the class, she barely looked up. Soft-voiced and gentle, she was the loveliest creature Elisha had seen. Her face was rosy, and golden curls escaped the light blue satin band that matched the color of her eyes. As she demurely took her seat, Elisha admired her dainty profile.

He put a flask filled with violets beside her inkwell the next morning. He waited for the moment when her large blue eyes flew open and she put her button nose into his fragrant bouquet. When she looked around the room and discreetly measured him, Elisha looked away.

At recess he didn't dare speak to the girl, though White Gloves approached her every chance he got.

Then one blissful day she invited Elisha to meet her parents and escort her to singing school. A flustered but happy Elisha slicked back his hair and took himself down to a Cheap John store. The purchase of a coat set him back a precious $15, which meant he'd go on short rations for months. But he considered his purchase worthwhile. Anything for Rosie! (Elisha called her "Rosie", though this was not her real name.)

At the appointed hour, he mounted the porch steps of a cottage set in a garden surrounded by a white picket fence. Wildflowers trembled in his hands, and he hoped he wasn't going to stutter.

The girl opened the door, smiling sweetly. Elisha stepped into a carpeted room. He gaped at overstuffed furniture, a piano, a what-not, and a table with carved legs. Dazzled by the splendor, he scarcely heard Rosie's cooing voice.

"Oh, how nice of you to bring these fragrant flowers. My parents aren't back from the city yet, but I guess you know this gentleman."

A slender youth stepped into the room. Elisha froze. *White Gloves!*

"Glovie" pushed and punched Elisha out the door and down the porch steps. "Don't you ever bring flowers again!" he hissed.

Elisha clutched his bleeding face. Then picking himself up, he limped through the garden gate, the girl's laughter following after him as Rosie and White Gloves ambled down the lane.

"What happened to you?" Elijah exclaimed, staring at his brother.

"She invited me for mischief, brother." Elisha tossed his $15 coat onto his bunk and dashed cold water on his swelling face. "She set me up, she and her white-gloved friend."

"I've had it!" Elijah exploded. "Let's go back to the mountains and be done with this place."

Chapter Five
Marksmen

The morning after his "date" with Rosie, Elisha knocked at Mr. Burlingame's office. As he waited for an invitation to enter, Elijah poked him and pointed. "The Latin teacher is coming. He'll miss us in class."

The Latin teacher strode down the hall toward them, then stopped and contemplated Elisha's bruised face. "How did this happen? Did you injure yourself?"

"I, uh—" Elisha stammered.

"Did it happen at work?"

"N-not at work." Elisha turned and knocked again. Why didn't Mr. Burlingame open the door?

"Our president left for Petaluma on school business," the teacher explained. "Let us hurry ere the bell strikes." He strode toward the classroom beside the twins.

Instead of introducing the lesson for the day, the teacher said, "I invite all of you to my church next Sunday. I shall deliver a sermon about freeing the Black man."

The Latin teacher was Healdsburg's Methodist preacher and an eloquent Republican. Unlike other professors at the academy, he boldly showed his clean-shaven face. His massive head revealed strength, an impression that was reinforced by his powerful shoulders. When his fist struck the desk or his voice thundered, he was as forceful as the toughest circuit rider in the mines. "Thunderhead," pupils called him.

Elisha admired his teacher. A learned man from Eastern colleges, this scholar and fine penman had cultivated a modulated voice. Dropping from great heights, he would lower his voice to an awed whisper when relating a tender story from the Scriptures. The man was devoted to his faith, parishioners, and pupils. The gaze of his sharp blue eyes silenced any but the most rebellious troublemaker. That's why it came as a surprise to Elisha when White Gloves rose and challenged the seasoned man.

"Are you for, or against, freeing the slaves?" Glovie asked, without so much as adding the customary "sir."

"I am for freeing the Black man," the teacher asserted. "I sense an undeniable movement toward secession in California. We must not allow separation to happen for, as Mr. Abraham Lincoln stated in his simple but forceful prose, 'A house divided against itself cannot stand.'"

Glovie stuck out his chin. "My pater and his associates will attend your sermon, if only to give you a different opinion." The young man's lip curled. "Pater says we will secede from the Union and join the Southern States. Our relatives are gentlemen plantation owners who need slaves to harvest their cotton."

"Hear, hear!" Glovie bowed to his friends' foot-stomping approval, reveling in his new prominence.

Then Rosie raised her hand and stood upon receiving the teacher's nod. "Losing slaves would hurt Southern planters, just as it would local dairy farmers who lost their cowherds." She sat down, blushing to the approving chuckles of classmates.

The teacher had been following the exchange in tight-lipped silence. "Secession is wrong," he emphasized. "We must preserve the Union and free the Black man. Most of all, we must do it without bloodshed."

He addressed Glovie. "I invite your father and his friends to hear my sermon. I can promise a lively meeting."

Elisha raised his hand.

"Yes, Mr. Brooks?"

Elisha stood up, wishing he could hide his bruised face, his too-short sleeves, his high-water trousers. "Black men do more than harvest cotton," he said. "For example, Black men ferried our ox team and wagon, as well as my mother and us six children across the swollen Missouri. If it hadn't been for their courage and skill, we might not have survived. Another Black man saved my family from starvation. My brother and I are alive, thanks to this Black man."

"How did this happen, Mr. Brooks?"

"Our last two oxen, my Indian pony, and Father's mule pulled our wagon up the eastern side of the Sierra Nevada. Ours was the last wagon of the 1852 migration. We were out of food and trying to outrun a blizzard. Father directed us over a pass that was lower and easier to negotiate than the terrible Donner Pass. A Black man had discovered the pass only a year earlier."

"Are you speaking of Mr. James Beckwourth?" the teacher interrupted.

"Yes, sir. Jim—I mean Mr. Beckwourth—fed us vegetables from his kitchen garden and gave us a warm place to sleep. Thanks to him, we reached our winter shelter and survived." Elisha's face throbbed, and the swelling impaired his vision. He sighed with relief when Elijah raised his hand and stood up.

"Jim gave us children sweetmeats, and he let my little brothers ride in front of him on his horse. He told wonderful stories of his life with the Indians. Though he was Black, he spoke like a Southern gentleman. People around Bidwell Bar called Jim's house the 'Emigrants' Landing Place.'"

The Latin teacher nodded. "I have heard of Mr. Beckwourth's amazing generosity. After discovering the low pass over the Sierra Nevada, this gentleman improved the road and opened a hostelry near the mountain pass that bears his name. This Black man saved countless weary, wayworn emigrants. His merciful deeds will long be remembered." The teacher's eyes softened. "Sometimes a more generous heart lies imbedded in the body of a runaway slave than beats in the chest of a free man who professes to be a good Christian." His gaze measured Glovie, who had shrunk into his seat. "Never will we send these unfortunate slaves back to their cruel masters. Free or slave, Black or White, we are children of God."

Elisha turned to the window. A horse and buggy clattered up the drive. He knew the driver by the way the wheels turned around the bend. It was Mr. Burlingame, driving with his usual zip. Dressed in suit, cravat, and high top hat, he made a dashing figure. He nudged his brother. "Mr. Burlingame is back."

Latin class over, the twins rushed into the hall with the others. More agitation than they'd ever encountered in this hall churned up the classmates.

Glovie elbowed his way through the crowd. "The preacher wants to free the slaves," he taunted. "Doesn't he know where we come from? Tell your parents to be at the church and hear his sermon. Let's smash Thunderhead to pulp."

"Hear, hear!"

Elisha's face clouded in a frown. "The preacher is going to be in bad shape, brother." He led the way to the president's office. Mr. Burlingame's "Enter" yielded to a shocked exclamation. "Have you been in a fight, Elisha?"

Elisha fidgeted. He wasn't keen on confessing his defeat. He'd acted like a greenhorn. "It's nothing, sir." He ignored Elijah's astonished look. "We've come to see you about the Latin teacher."

"We *have?*" Elijah's jaw dropped.

Elisha stepped on his brother's toes to shut him up.

A smile erupted on Mr. Burlingame's face. "What about the Latin teacher?"

"I'm worried about him, for he might get hurt," Elisha said.

Mr. Burlingame laughed out loud. "If anyone can take care of himself, it's your Latin teacher."

"They're going to lynch him come Sunday," Elisha predicted. "He has invited the entire town to hear his sermon about freeing the Black man."

"Dear me!" Mr. Burlingame jumped up. "They'll tear him to pieces and throw him to the wolves."

"We didn't come here to talk about the Latin teacher!" Elijah protested. "We came to put in our resignation. You best hire new janitors, Mr. Burlingame. We've taken enough abuse. Look at Elisha! If our mother saw him like this she'd rise from her grave."

"It's the fellow with the white gloves and the blond girl from San Francisco, isn't it?"

Mr. Burlingame's keen observation astounded Elisha. "How did you know?"

"I saw it coming." Mr. Burlingame paced the floor. "Now you've given me two problems to solve." He stopped. "Can the two of you stay on for another week until I find a replacement? I shall deal with the Latin teacher first."

Elisha poked his brother, who looked sullen.

Mr. Burlingame brightened. "We'll change your image, starting today. The brash young fellows in this school are cowards at heart. They haven't had your training. We'll beat them." He grinned. "What do you suggest we do?" he challenged Elisha.

"My brother and I will be glad to protect our teacher," Elisha blurted.

Elijah objected. "Are you crazy? There's going to be a lynch mob."

"We survived the San Francisco waterfront," Elisha reminded him.

On the day of the sermon, Elisha heaped his best pebbles on the table. The church bell rang. Men in carriages and horseback riders headed for the church on the corner of Fitch and Hayden Streets.

Elijah grumbled. "He's a big man. Let him take care of himself. I want to get back home alive."

"No, Elijah, we must think of our teacher. He's helping folks like Jim. We'd be dead if Jim hadn't helped us." Elisha heaped his brother's pebbles on top of his own.

Elijah sighed. "Mother always said an extra prayer for Jim, but she wasn't fond of fights."

Elisha knew how much his twin missed Mother. He himself felt an ever-present ache. Sometimes the ache was dull; sometimes it throbbed like a toothache. He spoke softly. "Mother wanted us to be safe, Elijah, and she'd want our teacher to be safe."

"Why does he have to give that stupid sermon? Why does he invite the entire town?" Elijah grumbled. "The

Trout-Lilly
Addler's-Jongue
Erythronium americanum

Southeners will attack him, and he'll fight to the end. Only a fool does that, if you ask me. He knows he can't win against a mob."

"He's following his conscience, Elijah. There's more to life than looking out for number one."

Elijah scraped up his pebbles and dropped them into his pocket.

People milled about the church's picket fence and climbed the wooden steps leading to the double doors. Normally, children romped about and the adults acted dignified. Children were absent today. The few women present wore aprons and ample skirts. They were unlike Rosie's mother, who was dainty and elegant. Seasoned pioneers, these women might enjoy watching a fight.

In contrast, the men wore suits and cravats, the formal attire worn by business and professional men. Some gentlemen had brought their hired men, tough guys, not unlike body guards.

Glovie stood aside, telling jokes and enjoying his friends' bursts of laughter. Elisha resented the carnival atmosphere and the men's ugly remarks as they speculated on the preacher's upcoming talk.

As far as he could tell, nobody was armed. A mob didn't need weapons to single out a victim and do him in, he reckoned. Hands in pockets, Elisha strolled toward the church beside his twin. A whisper rippled through Glovie's crowd.

"It's them—the marksmen from the mines. They never miss!"

Mr. Burlingame had spread word of the twins' unfailing marksmanship with pebbles. Upon his advice, the twins had practiced target hitting with pebbles in front of awestruck blabbermouths. Back in Bidwell Bar, the twins' well-aimed pebbles had protected their bovine charges from wild beasts.

Elisha boldly showed his face. Approaching the wooden church with its bell tower projecting from the windowless facade, he suddenly remembered his father. The church was a somber structure, the work of Eastern carpenters. Pa couldn't have built it sturdier. He missed an able-bodied father by his side, but Pa was an invalid. His chest heaved. Nobody showed respect for Pa, though people recalled Mother with respect.

"Coulda had any man she chose. Great woman, your mother," they said.

Elisha wished his father were like the Latin teacher, a man of conviction, who gladly fought for what he believed was true and right.

Elijah poked him in the ribs. "Wake up, brother. This is no time for daydreaming."

Chapter Six
Lynch Mob at Church

The Latin teacher fired verbal thunderbolts into the rowdy gathering. Hecklers offered laughs and ugly remarks, making a mockery of the church. Up front, in plain view, Elisha kept his eagle eye on the slightest movement. The sunlight streamed through the four tall side windows, providing good light. His sweaty hand rested lightly on the pebbles in his pocket, ready.

Beside him, Elijah jumped whenever a heckler taunted the preacher. "It wouldn't take much for a mob like this to string up the preacher and us too," he whispered.

The church had turned into a place to boo the villain and cheer the hero. Only the "villain" stood in the pulpit, and the "heroes" sat in the pews. Glovie's father obviously relished a battle. Tall, and dressed in the latest style, he looked like his son, only heavier, and he threw his weight around. He had money to lend and jobs to give. He had friends, people who sought his favor, and paid servants.

I'd hate to work for Glovie's father, Elisha thought. *I'd rather go back to stripping bark.*

The big man raised his voice against the preacher. "You

say that slavery is the most damning thing against us. Well, sir, if you don't like the way we conduct business, you'd best get out of California for we shall secede." Glovie's father was getting steamed.

"I challenge you, sir," the Latin teacher fired back. "There should not be one Christian in this church in sympathy with secession and a possible civil war."

Glovie's father turned toward the congregation and shouted, "All Christians in favor of secession, please rise!"

More people stood and roared approval than remained in their seats. Elisha gripped a pebble in his fist, ready to hurl the missile. Tempers rose to a fever pitch, and still the preacher stood his ground.

"Those of you who favor secession are playing into the hands of the devil!" he thundered. "Let us free the Black man, our brother, so he can believe that Christ also died for him. Let us break the shackles of the slave!"

"Yeah, let's free the poor suckers!" a woman near the door screeched. "I'm gettin' outta here, and you folks better respect our preacher." She walked out, and other women followed her in haste. With the women gone, the men became intolerably aggressive.

Then a giant of a man, who had come in late and sat silently near the exit, pressed through men crowding the aisle. Colorless eyes under heavy brows showed neither passion nor hate. The collar of his coarse shirt gaped open, revealing a hairy chest. Wordlessly, he reached into his coat pocket and pulled out a length of rope. He held up a noose in front of the pulpit. "This is what the likes of you get, preacher!" he boomed.

The preacher faced the giant squarely. "You can hang me and please your master, but you will never stop justice and truth, sir. Take me, if you dare! I am yours to do with as you wish, if it be God's will."

Elisha's adams apple jumped nervously in his throat. Power, the Latin teacher had *power!* To offer his life because he valued a human being took courage—and a heap of compassion.

"Stand back!" Elisha heard his own cracking voice. He maneuvered himself in front of the giant. "Stand back, if you know what's good for you!" he commanded.

His brother's voice sounded strong behind him. "All of you, clear this church if you want to live. We'll have no lynching here! Whoever touches the preacher reckons with us!"

A murmur swept through the church. "It's them—the marksmen from the mines—they never miss!" Fainthearted souls scrambled for the exit. Glovie and friends scurried outside. The giant stared at Elisha, appearing confused. Elisha stood firm, his heart pounding. "Drop the rope and leave, unless you want to die for your master."

To his amazement, the giant obeyed his command. He dropped the rope and stomped outside, avoiding his master's scathing look. Glovie's father cursed and exited. With the ringleader gone, the others soon dispersed.

Elisha felt faint.

"Good work, brother!" Elijah praised him.

Elisha stepped onto the riverboat's swaying plank, carefully carrying the book box. Behind him, Elijah balanced the books they had taken out to lighten the load. "Careful! Don't drop them," Elisha warned.

"I won't. "

A classmate driving a team and wagon had transported the twins' books from Healdsburg to Sacramento. Now the steamship was about to carry books and graduates upriver to Marysville. The cost of passage cut into the twins' meager finances, but they knew of no other way to get their books home.

The steamer's colorful banners fluttered in the morning breeze. Baggage and passengers crowded the vessel. The

twins found a quiet corner and sorted through their precious books. Finally, the boilers got going, the calliope
whistle shrilled, and they pulled away from the shore. Two
tall smoke stacks belched out black smoke, and the huge
paddle wheel on the ship's side made splashing sounds.

Elijah put the last book into the box. "I want to look
around, brother. Why don't you watch our books for now?"

"We'll take turns," Elisha agreed. "Don't be long."

Elijah took his time. Elisha's stomach growled; he was
famished. At long last, his brother returned.

"I was lucky," Elijah beamed. "The cook let me chop
wood for my meal. He says you can come and eat, too. He
has the best food!"

Elisha gulped. He didn't remember when he had
been more hungry. "Does he have any more wood to
chop, Elijah?"

"No, I chopped it all."

"Then I can't accept the cook's offer, because I haven't
earned it."

Elijah frowned. "Don't be silly!"

"No, accepting something for nothing isn't right."

"Go tell the cook!" Elijah insisted.

Elisha trudged downstairs, where tantalizing odors from
the ship's galley assaulted his senses. "Do you have work
for me?" he asked the cook.

The cook stared. "Why, you just chopped my wood."

"I'm the other twin," Elisha explained. "I can't accept the
meal you offered because I haven't earned it." He trudged
back, trying to forget the enticing aromas. His stomach had
clamored for food during the entire trip. He scolded himself
for being such a wolfish creature.

While his brother dozed on the bench, Elisha refigured
their finances. At the end of their six-month term, they had
had $5.25 left. Transport of the books to Sacramento had
cost $2.50. The steamship passage to Marysville set them
back another $2.50. Only the long walk from Healdsburg

to Sacramento and sleeping in the lee of rocks or trees had been free.

With the last 25 cents, the twins bought supper for the starving Elisha, and another small loaf of bread for breakfast and dinner the next day. A haymow provided free lodging.

On their 40-mile march home from Marysville, the twins grinned at seeing two conspicuous cones rising above the valley floor. Growing out of the level plain of the Sacramento Valley, the buttes looked like twins a volcano had belched out in good humor. Elisha and Elijah looked at each other and laughed. Butte County was well named, they agreed.

Suddenly lighthearted, they discussed recent happenings. After the church incident, the situation had improved for the "marksmen from the mines." The twins got respect from pupils who spurned Glovie's clique.

An outing to Mount St. Helena with three professors and a friendly student provided an exciting highlight. Elisha knew he'd long cherish the memory of fun, learning, and nature appreciation. The outing celebrated six months of concentrated study and menial work.

Having acquired a taste for study, Elisha wanted to go on to college. Professors had spoken highly of Yale and Harvard, but Elisha sighed. He'd need $1,000 for travel money to reach the Atlantic coast by way of Cape Horn. He shuddered at taking a sea voyage, and he dreaded a 3,000-mile overland journey.

Once in the foothills, the twins inhaled the sweet fragrance of pines. As they neared their father's cottage they felt footsore but glad, for they had gained an education.

Father hobbled out to greet them, and the twins asked about their younger brothers.

Father's report was short. "Folks are taking care of Jay and Joseph. The other boys are working and supporting me."

Elisha voiced his anguish. "Why must our family be separated, Pa? Will my brothers remember the Brooks family? Will they remember Mother?"

Father appeared angry and sad. He pulled a letter from a cupboard and handed the crackling parchment to Elisha. "Read this letter!"

"Who sent it?" Elisha turned to the last page. "'Written August lst 1860 by J. H. Zumwalt,'"he read. "Why, it's from John!"

"Read!" Father commanded.

Elisha's blood chilled on reading the first sentence: "'The sickness and death of my darling wife Vienna . . .'" A knife twisted inside him as he recalled the vivacious image of his sister.

"Read on," Father urged.

Elisha's voice cracked. "'Of her sickness before her speedy change there can be but little said. Her disease being childbed fever continued from Thursday July 19th until July 29th about the same. On Sunday 29 about two o'clock she desired me to write to her father and have him come and see her.'"

Elisha interrupted himself. "Did you see her, Pa?"

"No." Father looked stricken.

Elisha continued John's long letter. "'She seemed quite anxious and fearful that her father would not come in time to see her, thus she remained about the same until she called me to her and said, "I cannot live but very little longer. I'll soon go." Then she said, "If you think my sins are not forgiven, pray for me for I would pray night and day if I thought they were not." I told her that the Lord would be merciful.

"'She wished to see her father and brothers and sang the hymn, "We'll stand the storm; it won't be long." This she repeated three times, then our friends gathered around her, weeping, when she turned her head and said in a plain, gentle tone, "Dear friends, don't weep for me." She said that her bed was so soft and nice, for "Jesus can make a dying bed as soft as downy pillows are." Then she asked us to sing something, and we sang.

" 'O, sing to me of heaven
    When I am called to die.' "

Elisha blew his nose and his twin wept loudly.

"Read on," Father urged.

" 'She told me to tell her little boy that his mother died happy in a Saviour's love, that he must live a good life and then meet her in heaven. During the night she expressed a desire to see my brother Joseph, then it seemed as if those were the only wishes ungratified to see her Father and my brother Joseph. On the morning of the 30th, her life was so far spent that she could only lisp "John" distinctly enough to be understood. Her tongue soon grew stiff, her eyes were closed, and she was soon found sleeping in death with a smile on her face, a plain expressive smile.' "

Tears rolled down Elisha's cheeks. "Where were we when all this happened?"

"In the mines, scraping up money for Healdsburg," Elijah sobbed.

Anger gripped Elisha. "Why did this happen, Pa? Why did they let our sister die? Mother had eight babies and she survived. Mother always knew what to do. This wouldn't have happened if our mother had been at Vienna's bedside. Imagine, dying at 21 years of age and leaving a baby behind!"

Father nodded.

"What will happen to the baby, Pa?" Elisha asked.

"He's a Zumwalt, son. John and his mother are raising him for now. If John gets married again, his new wife will be the only mother he knows."

"It's not fair, Pa. Vienna's baby is our baby too!"

Father shook his head. "A baby needs a woman's care. Your mother knew how to raise babies. She fussed over all you children." He sniffled. "You boys were a lot for your mother to handle until Vienna was big enough to help. That girl made a great nursemaid. She was the best."

Elijah stooped down and picked up rocks and threw

them. "Vienna would have been better off being a teacher. She could have been a schoolmarm and lived a long life."

"Some swain would have snatched her off," Father said. "She was too pretty. She could have stayed with me—we could have managed, she and I."

The desolation in Father's voice told Elisha where Vienna's death had hit hardest. The father who had treated his sons harshly grieved the loss of his only daughter.

Mother's admonition rang in Elisha's ear. "You must respect your father, Elisha. It's the law of God."

Chapter Seven
A Teacher's Certificate

Whoa!"

Elisha stopped his four-horse team beside a mountain meadow. He set the brakes, then jumped off and blocked the wheels. A quick check showed that the freight was securely fastened. He was hauling a load from Oroville to the American Valley by way of the Bidwell Bar suspension bridge. Ahead lay the steep canyon road that passed the Berry Creek location, where his father's sawmill had been washed away during the family's first winter in California.

After watering the horses and freeing them to graze, Elisha sat down on a mossy rock. Pine branches shielded him from the high summer sun. He pulled bread from his basket and opened the textbook he had brought along to study in preparation for an upcoming teacher's examination. Ever since his return from Healdsburg months before, he had made good use of his time.

He munched his lunch, engrossed in his study. Birds streaked through green canopies in the fresh mountain air. A breaking of dry branches broke Elisha's concentration. Then he saw a pair of long horns appear over the crest of the hill as a huge black ox trotted into view. The ox snorted on seeing him and began pawing the ground. Elisha jumped.

"Brock! Old Brockleface! Is that you?" he yelled.

The ox raised his head, as if listening.

"It's me, Elisha, your good, old friend!" Elisha calmed the horses and prayed the ox wouldn't charge.

The ox stretched out his neck and bellowed.

"Come under Brock!" Elisha called. Holding up an imaginary yoke, he advanced until he stood near the ox. Slowly and deliberately, the ox swung his long horns as if ready to go under the wooden yoke.

"Dear Brockleface!" Elisha stroked the ox's coarse hide. Years had passed since Brock had pulled the family's covered wagon. Tears stung Elisha's eyes. Many times he had looked for his pet. On freight hauling trips over the Sierra Nevada he wondered about Brock. When late snows blocked the road and he packed mules and donkeys over mountain trails, he worried how Brock kept warm. Handling a six-mule team and jerk line, sometimes climbing to heights of 7,000 feet, he looked for a trace of Brock.

Several times he had passed the clearing in which Nig, Brock's teammate, lay buried. Always he remembered Brock, the Michigan ox, they'd had to leave in the mountains. No yoke had touched Brock's neck in all these years. No hand had ruffled his coarse hair, for the ox had become shy of humans.

"Dear Brock, you're all alone," Elisha commiserated. "I know how you feel. You lost Nig, and I lost Mother and Vienna. We're both sad."

The ox's long, drawn-out bellow echoed in Elisha ears long after he drove away.

———

Elisha brushed off his $15 coat. He entered the examination room filled with eager youths and seasoned teachers alike, all anxious to obtain a teacher's certificate. His heart pounded at the sight of the five interrogators. These gentlemen, sitting around the large table, reminded Elisha of courtroom judges. He observed the one who asked the leading questions. A clipped mustache graced his upper lip, and receding hair formed a halo around his head. Sideburns grew down to his chin. A smile flitted about his lips when he got correct answers. His brown eyes looked out above spectacles perched low on his nose, boring into the person he was interrogating.

Another examiner sat motionless as an owl. Only his head moved, locating his prey. Small, wire-rimmed glasses covered the sockets of his eyes, reflecting the light as he moved his head. One never knew what tricky question he'd come up with next. When he glared at Elisha through his wire-rimmed spectacles, the boy shriveled. The examiner sniffed out his slightest hesitation, his thin, tight lips forbidding opposition. Paper rustled ominously as he leafed through the pages in front of him.

Elisha perspired under the collar of the white shirt he had bought for this important occasion. He couldn't tell whether he had passed or not.

Following recess, the examiners reappeared. The first name was called. "Eggleston."

A young man sprang up. "Here, sir!"

"You passed." Eggleston received his parchment.

"T. W. Bliss."

"Yes, sir! Thank you most kindly, sir." Bliss, an experienced Butte County teacher, accepted his certificate with expressions of gratitude.

"William Young."

"Here, sir! Much obliged." Young hugged his certificate, beaming like a clown.

Elisha shivered. A single certificate was left in the interrogator's hand.

"Elisha Brooks."

"Yes, sir!" Elisha felt faint. The parchment would permit

him to fulfill his mother's fondest dream.

The examiners, Mr. Osbourne, Mr. Wells, Mr. Chesney, Mr. Coughey, and the "ex officio" gave brief talks, after which four certified teachers walked out into the hot September sun. Elisha was disappointed not to see his twin brother, but Elijah had found a job and probably couldn't get away. He hoped Elijah would take the exam the following year.

Elisha shifted his bundle from one bony shoulder to the other. The September sun scorched the hills of the gold country. Damp hair clung to his forehead, and his shoulder blades felt wet. He fanned himself in the shade of a mountain laurel. A jay fluttered screeching from branch to branch. Elisha imitated the bird's call, a trick he had learned from Indian playmates.

He continued his march to the hamlet of Enterprise in the neighboring Mountain Springs school district, where folks had built a brand-new schoolhouse. He found the trustees and followed them to the cabin astride the water ditch. The one-room schoolhouse was sparsely furnished with benches, a crude desk, and a barrel that served as the teacher's seat. He listened to water sounds from beneath the building and inhaled the aroma of freshly-cut lumber while the trustees discussed an eight-month term. He imagined students sitting on the benches, but it was the whiskey barrel teacher's seat that threw him. Could he start his career on *that*?

"Tell us if you want the job, young fellow. The pay isn't much, seein' that you haven't done any teachin' before," said a burly man.

"I want the job, but—"

"But what?" The burly man scowled. "I hope we won't have any trouble with you. All we need is a sassy young fellow telling us grown men what to do."

The speaker was a toughened miner. He and the others had come West the hard way, Elisha knew. Some had crossed the Plains in covered wagons. Others had braved the fever-ridden Isthmus of Panama on muleback, or rounded Cape Horn in storm-tossed sailing vessels. Having weathered such odds, they weren't likely to respect the objections of a beardless youth, he feared.

The great gold rush of 1849 lay more than a dozen years behind. The gold was giving out, and miners were turning to farming and business for a livelihood. Families had followed the gold seekers to the rough-and-tumble mining camps. Now it was time the children got some schooling.

One of the trustees cleared his throat. "If we're to support the school, we expect your cooperation, young man."

Elisha's eyes snapped. "I shan't start my teaching career sitting on a whiskey barrel, sir."

"It's the barrel or nothin'," the burly man boomed.

Elisha's jaw tightened. He remembered how young miners got killed in drunken brawls, how drunkards made women miserable and gave children a hard time. Accept a whiskey barrel as his official seat? Showcase the despised emblem in front of tender young eyes? Start his teaching on a compromise? No, it wasn't right.

A simple yes would make everybody happy, he realized. This was the year he hoped would mark a milestone in his life. He had prepared for this important step, had sacrificed, starved, even risked his life for it.

"Your answer!" the trustee urged.

Elisha gulped. The image of his mother surfaced in his mind, a brown-haired woman with searching, compelling eyes. She had taught him the difference between right and wrong. His answer came almost against his will. "Not on a whiskey barrel, sir!" Sweat beads trickled over his brows. Was he losing the first big chance of his life? He felt lightheaded. His knees buckled and he keeled over. Muscled arms laid him out on the plank floor.

"Let's give the lad a break," one of the trustees suggested. "He looks like he hasn't eaten all day. I'll send the wife over with biscuits. He'll change his mind when he gets some food in his stomach."

The men left, boots thumping on the hard-packed ground. A fly buzzed about the room, stopping on Elisha's nose, then on the whiskey barrel, before zooming outside. Water sounds grew loud, gurgling at first, then rushing and pounding. Elisha stirred and stared.

"Ma, Ma! He's coming to!" two boyish voices cried.

A woman hovered over him. She was plump and pink-faced with straw blond hair pulled back from her round face. She put her arm under him and trickled cool water over his lips. "The men are mad at you," she said. "They say you're a rabble-rouser."

"I'm no rabble-rouser, ma'am, but they want me to sit on that whiskey barrel." Elisha pushed her tin cup away.

She looked dumbfounded. "Why is that so bad? Our children need a teacher. Say you changed your mind and you'll have a job." The woman's marble eyes evaluated him. She held her tongue as Elisha looked up at her. Wordlessly, she handed him a biscuit.

After he had eaten, she said, "Well?"

Elisha pointed to the barrel. "Not on that, ma'am. Young children mustn't be exposed to such a sight."

"Why not? It's an empty barrel. One barrel is as good as another."

"There's nothing good about children being reminded of whiskey every hour of the school day, ma'am. Whiskey is bad for people. Children mustn't see their teacher on that barrel or they'll grow up thinking it's all right to drink liquor."

The woman sighed. "You've got somethin' there, lad. Whiskey's put many a young man into his grave. People get to fightin' and a gun goes off." She pushed the two tow-heads away from her. "Go git your pa and tell the kids school's a startin'."

"But ma'am!" Elisha objected.

"Don't worry yourself none. I kin handle menfolk."

The towheads ran outside and soon returned with a man whose name Elisha remembered. Mr. Crandall carried a manly head on his loose frame. He worked outdoors, judging by his pale forehead and the bronzed lower part of his face. He was a man with lean cheeks and clear eyes that faced a person squarely. Not an immoderate man, Elisha judged, not a drunkard.

"So you've come around," he addressed Elisha, looking pleased. "The whiskey barrel stays."

"No, it doesn't!" his wife retorted. "It's bad enough that our kids pass the saloon on their way to school. It's bad enough that young men get killed in gunfights. The barrel goes out. I won't have my Dan and Jeremy look at it all day while they learn the three R's."

She upended the barrel and rolled it out the door. A swift kick of her boot sent it tumbling into the water ditch. Satisfied, she rubbed her hands. "This young feller is right for the job," she asserted. "He'll do fine."

Mr. Crandall kept a straight face. "Go find yourself a box, young man."

Elisha hurried outside. From a stack of discarded boxes behind a merchant's establishment, he selected a good one. Carrying the trophy to the schoolhouse, he beckoned the town's children to come along.

"Hurrah, we've got ourselves a teach!" A gang of boys and girls cheered.

Elisha lifted one child after another onto the box as he got his or her name and age. He rejoiced. God had entrusted him with children that had gone uneducated for too long. Putting down the last child, Elisha remembered his mother, Eliza Ann Brooks, who had been the first schoolteacher of Butte County, California, and smiled happily to himself.

Chapter Eight
Boys in Blue

Every school day during his eight-month term at Enterprise, Elisha opened with the Bible and closed with prayer. Monday mornings he gave an exercise in reading the Scriptures. He dedicated the remaining hours to basic subjects.

At the end of the term, he left behind notes to help a rookie teacher get started the following fall. Then he hoisted books, bedroll, and cooking pans onto his shoulder and found himself a summer job. Hauling freight to neighboring Plumas County provided a change of pace. Wherever he loaded or unloaded goods, people talked about secession from the Union, a subject that upset Elisha.

In the autumn, he learned of the need for a teacher in the nearby hamlet of Wyandotte. He applied and was hired. For eight busy months, Elisha drilled students who sadly lacked knowledge of the three R's and the Word of God.

"If you don't learn to read, how will you know what's in the Scriptures?" Elisha challenged boys who saw nothing in reading. "How can you read the newspaper, a letter your mother sends you, or pass an exam to get promoted at work?

"If you don't learn to write, how can you pen a letter to a friend? If you don't learn how to count, how do you know what things cost? How do you know how much money your boss is paying you?" At the end of the term, Elisha saw with satisfaction that even the slowest student demonstrated progress.

He packed his bundle, careful not to crush the wooden box containing his dried wildflowers. He visited Father, handed over his earnings, then hired himself out as a teamster.

"Secession!" The word popped up everywhere. Civil war was raging in the East, and Elisha wanted to help. On November 15, 1864, he joined the California Volunteers, expecting to be sent to the front. Four days later, he was mustered into service at Fort Point at San Francisco.

The fort perched at the edge of the stormy channel called Golden Gate. Built in the shape of a ship and modeled after Fort Sumter in South Carolina, the massive brick bastion prided itself in being the largest fortification on the West Coast. Its roof and gun ports sported muzzle-loading cannon, capable of hurling cannon balls two miles across the water.

"No privateer trying to enter the Bay and control California's gold will make it past this place," the first sergeant joked.

Shivering in wind, rain, and sea fog, Elisha marvelled at the fort's jutting brick bastions, circular stone stairways and passageways resounding with bugle calls. Under his youthful commander, Captain Morgan S. Grover, Elisha became part of the 8th Regiment, Company D. His outfit of 68 men promptly lost 17 men to desertion, including four cooks. Captain Grover summoned Elisha, who wondered what he had done wrong.

"I have been watching you, private," the commander began. "You're younger than most men, but they seem to listen to you. How would you like to serve as chaplain?"

Elisha gasped. "I have no rank, sir."

"That can be changed. Let me talk to the colonel," the captain offered. "In the meantime, talk to the men. We cannot save the Union with deserters."

The private was promoted to the rank of second lieutenant and served as chaplain. Then the war suddenly ended. Elisha was mustered out on February 6, 1865, and left the fort, stunned. All those cannon had never fired a shot in anger. His three-year enrollment had lasted only three months. Had he done his share? Had he done enough to free the slaves?

Thrown into the streets of San Francisco, he was destitute and unprepared for city life. All he had to show for his military time was a blue uniform, boots, a hat, and gloves with gauntlet cuffs. Where was a beardless fellow with neatly trimmed hair and a blue uniform to go? No haymow provided free shelter. No living off the land was possible. He walked without aim or plan. Spread out over steep sand hills he saw houses, not cozy cottages, but monster buildings several stories high.

"Not a tree in sight," he grumbled.

Plodding from house to house, asking for work, he had doors slammed in his face. Why were people so unfriendly? Then he met an acquaintance from Fort Point.

"How are you doing, buddy?" the fellow asked.

Elisha sighed. "Nobody seems to need a teacher or teamster in this city."

The fellow harumphed. "Don't you know that Frisco people despise boys in blue?"

"They do?" As Elisha stepped aside a passerby sneered at his uniform. Elisha meant to give the stranger a piece of his mind, but just then a carriage pulled by two beautiful black horses distracted him. Through the side window he glimpsed a woman who looked familiar. "I know that woman!" he exclaimed. "She's a farmer's wife from St. Joseph County, Michigan. We used to be neighbors. I know her!"

The passerby laughed. "A farmer's wife, eh? She's the

wife of a banker, and her daughter is married to a rich saloon owner."

Elisha had glimpsed a girl's tangle of red curls. Vienna's friend Priscilla had hair that shade of red! "What's the banker's name?" he asked.

"Graham." The man walked on. "A farm wife indeed," he muttered.

Elisha walked on in a daze. How could he mistake a prominent city lady for good old Mrs. Wilson? Memories came flooding back. He remembered how Mrs. Wilson had embraced Mother, bidding her a safe journey. Mother had said farewell with dignity and courage, then hoisted Elmont on her arm, where the toddler pulled at Mother's crocheted collar, trying to reach her brooch.

Day after day, Elisha asked hostile strangers for odd jobs. The pennies people gave him for his services barely kept him in food. One day he trudged up a steep street. The fog was lifting, revealing mansions clinging to a hillside. A buggy

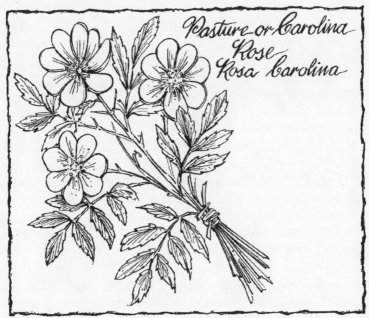

Pasture or Carolina Rose
Rosa Carolina

came careening downhill, the driver whipping his horse. Elisha jumped aside just in time to miss being run over.

"Stop!" the redhaired girl beside the driver screeched. The horse reared and the buggy came to a halt. "Did you hurt yourself?" she asked Elisha.

"I— well—" He rubbed his smarting behind.

"I see you were an officer," the redhead observed. "I thought officers were rich."

"Not all of them, ma'am." Elisha hurt, and the girl's question didn't help much.

"Why are you tramping up this steep hill?" demanded the driver, a slight young man.

Elisha swallowed his immediate dislike for the boyish driver. "I'm looking for work."

"What can you do?"

"Drive a team, herd cows, do farm work."

The driver smirked. "Check my saloons at the waterfront. I always can use a hand. Help doesn't last these days."

Elisha shook his head. The words "saloon" and "waterfront" offended him. He'd rather starve than mingle with drunkards. He preferred sleeping in alleyways to being dragged on a ship against his will.

"Can you do a clerk's duty?" The young driver sounded impatient.

"I can, and I'll think about your offer." Elisha limped away.

"Suit yourself," the driver called back.

The buggy careened away. The girl's laughter offended Elisha's ears. The redhead was the daughter of Mrs. Graham, the lady he had mistaken for Mrs. Wilson, he realized.

"I must be going crazy," he muttered. Why not go home to the mountains, where a fellow could make a living? *If I had money I'd book passage home today,* he told himself.

Home? But where was home? His brothers were scattered. Mother was gone; Vienna was gone. And Father was not likely to welcome a son who brought home no wages.

Chapter Nine
Job at the Mint

Elisha steadied himself against the wall of an eating establishment. Food odors drifted out whenever customers entered or left the building. He had walked all morning, asking for odd jobs that would pay for a bite to eat. All doors seemed closed to the boy in blue. People all but spit in his face. At least the wall provided shelter against the stiff wind blowing from the Golden Gate and reflected the weak sun filtering through the overcast.

A gentleman in suit and top hat strode briskly toward the restaurant. Seeing Elisha, he stopped. "Are you all right, young man?"

"Y-yes, sir." Embarrassed to be seen in this weak condition, Elisha turned to leave.

"Wait!" the man called. "Don't I know you?"

"I don't think so."

He looked puzzled. "Didn't I see you in Oroville?"

"I used to sell wildflowers while attending the Oroville school."

"The flower boy! I knew you looked familiar. How long have you been in San Francisco?"

"Months." Elisha wished his stomach didn't growl.

"How are things going for you?"

"Not very well," Elisha admitted. "I can't seem to get a job here, and I have no money to leave."

"That's too bad."

"I didn't mean to complain, sir. It's not your problem."

"No need to call me sir. Mr. Cheeseman will do."

"Thank you, Mr. Cheeseman. Are you going back to Oroville soon?" Elisha asked hopefully.

Mr. Cheeseman laughed. "Not likely. I'll have you know that you are looking at the assistant United States treasurer. I had best stay near my post at the Mint."

"The U.S. Mint?" Elisha forgot his hunger pangs. "Is there a position open for a graduate from academy, one who also has a teacher's certificate?"

"Not for a teacher, but academy graduate will do. When can you start?"

"Right now!"

"Let's discuss things over lunch." Mr. Cheeseman ushered Elisha into the restaurant.

After a filling meal, Mr. Cheeseman took Elisha to the Mint and appointed him as his representative.

With his first pay, Elisha was able to exchange his uniform for city clothes. He joined the Young Men's Christian Association and availed himself of the cleaning services of a Celestial. Relieved of job hunting, he felt free to accept his coworkers' invitation to a boating excursion on the Bay. They were bachelors, and a carefree lot. On the gangplank, Elisha realized that the fellows had also invited girls.

A gaudy girl with snappy eyes smiled at him on the swaying boat. "You work at the Mint, don't you?" she asked.

"I, uh, have only just started," Elisha stuttered. He wasn't used to being spoken to by girls.

"What do you fellows do with all the gold that's stashed away in those vaults?" The girl tossed bread crumbs over the railing and laughed when saucy seagulls snapped them up.

"We coin double eagles, gold eagles, gold half eagles, and California gold quarter eagles," Elisha reported.

"There must be tons of gold at the Mint."

"I suppose." The girl's questions made Elisha uncomfortable.

"I just love gold," she raved.

"We also coin silver quarters and half dollars."

She shrugged. "Who cares about those?"

"People who go hungry do," Elisha asserted.

"Oh, now I have offended you." She tapped him with her fan. "You never need to go hungry." She stressed the word "you."

"Why is that?" Elisha asked.

She smiled sweetly. "No doubt you own a big house."

"No, I don't."

"Surely, you own a fine carriage," she persisted.

Elisha shook his head. "Not so much as a buggy. The horsecar will suffice should I need public transportation. I'm a great walker. I can walk many miles without getting tired. Walking is good for the body and it costs no money."

Her naughty eyes looked up at him. "You spend your days in a place filled with gold and you walk?"

"The gold isn't mine."

She giggled. "Couldn't you help yourself to a pocketful once in a while"

Elisha felt the blood drain from his face. "You mean, steal from my employer?"

"The government doesn't miss a few paltry coins. Think of what you can buy with money." She fanned herself, looking wicked.

Elisha stepped back in shock. "I should never steal from my employer! It isn't right."

"Then how are you going to get rich? Gold buys houses and carriages and every good thing in life. Why scrimp when there's all this gold around?" She swept past Elisha and smiled at one of his coworkers.

Elisha shook. He couldn't believe what was happening.

"What's wrong, Brooks?" a clerk asked. "You look positively white."

Elisha pointed. "That girl just asked me to steal gold from the Mint. Why would she do that?"

The clerk shrugged. "Frisco girls are money bags; everybody knows that."

"But stealing is wrong."

The clerk laughed. "Frisco girls are greedy little creatures. If you can't offer a carriage, house, or money, you're not much of a catch."

Elisha felt sick.

Studying a book that evening, as was his habit, he found his attention wandering. How was a poor boy going to get himself a bride? He was saving every penny for a place of his own. Where was the rare city girl willing to share a modest cottage with him? Not any girl would do, of course. She must be a God-fearing person, one he could trust.

"Money bags, mischief makers, tramps in finery," he raged. "Keep your hands off girls, or you'll get hurt."

One day when Mr. Cheeseman came back from lunch he approached Elisha's desk with a gentleman in tow. "Dr. Morrison, I want you to meet my representative, Elisha Brooks. Elisha is knowledgeable about the wildflowers of the Sierra Nevada, a subject in which you are interested."

Elisha put away his partially eaten sandwich and extended his hand. "What can I do for you, sir?"

"May I ask you questions about certain flowers?"

"Certainly." Elisha swallowed the last dry bite of his sandwich.

Dr. Morrison rattled off unfamiliar names. "What can you tell me about these flowers?" he asked.

"I, uh, never learned the true names of the flowers I picked in Butte County. However, I can tell you what they look like."

Dr. Morrison's face fell. "No, Elisha. I must see the specimens."

Elisha's hopes soared. "During my school days in Oroville I developed a great love for wildflowers," he said.

"Yes, of course." The doctor was putting on his top hat, making ready to leave.

Seeing his chance fading, Elisha spoke rapidly. "I dried some flowers and brought them with me to San Francisco during the Civil War."

"You brought flowers to the war?"

"I know it sounds strange, but I couldn't simply abandon *my* flowers."

"Why not?"

"I hoped I'd find somebody who can identify them for me."

"Can you show me the dried flowers?"

"Oh, yes! Can you tell me their real names?"

"Can you bring the collection tomorrow?" Dr. Morrison asked. "We could look at it during your lunch break."

The next day, Dr. Morrison fairly sailed toward Elisha's desk. Elisha pointed to his wooden treasure box. Dr. Morrison raised the lid and lifted delicate plants from layers of paper, making grunting noises. Elisha felt embarrassed. He was sorry he had brought the box. Dr. Morrison eased the flowers back into the box and closed the lid.

"We must show these specimens to Dr. Kellogg at the Academy of Sciences," he stated. "Can you come with me right now?"

Take his flowers to an academy? Elisha was dumbfounded. This Dr. Kellogg would laugh at him. He'd call him a fool. Nevertheless, Elisha put on his coat.

Dr. Albert Kellogg, a botanist of international fame, did not laugh as he studied Elisha's collection. The botanist announced the proper names of all the flowers. Not one of the names Elisha had given his flowers proved to be correct.

When Elisha prepared to leave, Dr. Kellogg put his

hand on the box. "You took good care of these flowers," the botanist praised him. "However, there is no telling what will happen in the future. You're a bachelor and unsettled. Even if you were married, I'd worry about children's curious little hands. I'd feel better to see this collection preserved here."

"At the Academy of Sciences?" Elisha gasped.

"Would you let us exhibit your fine collection for a while, so that interested parties may study it?"

Elisha praised God! Somebody shared his love for the flowers he had carried with him from place to place. "You may keep the box," he offered.

"You mean you are donating this precious collection?" Dr. Kellogg asked.

Elisha nodded.

Before long, a letter arrived on Elisha's desk. Noting the letterhead and fine penmanship, Elisha read it carefully. Suddenly, he let out a "Whoopie!"

The clerk at the next desk looked up. "What happened?"

"Dr. Kellogg recommended me for membership in the Academy of Sciences," Elisha exulted. "My wildflowers are on permanent display at the academy's herbarium under the label 'Butte County flora'."

"Can I go see them?" the clerk asked.

"You can, I can, anybody can!"

Chapter Ten
Nellie

People milled around the churchyard, exchanging greetings and the latest news. Elisha had attended services with Gus, a fellow he had met at the Young Men's Christian Association. Gus never missed a chance to approach a pretty girl and was chatting with a bearded man and a blond girl.

Shivering in the stiff breeze, he signaled to Gus, hoping to get his roommate's attention. Who were these people? he wondered. The older man looked formidable, despite the florid color showing around his artfully trimmed beard. The girl's back was to him, but her occasional laugh sounded musical, Elisha thought.

Gus waved, indicating he'd soon be leaving. The girl turned around, her puzzled expression yielding to a bright smile. Was she smiling at him? Blood rushed to Elisha's face and he quickly looked away.

When he looked her way again, he saw that the older man had put a protective arm around the girl. "Come, Ellen, let's go home."

Elisha couldn't miss the gruffness in the man's voice nor the girl's curious expression as she turned and looked his way once more.

Gus strutted toward Elisha. "Sorry to make you wait."

"When will you quit chasing girls?" Elisha scolded.

"When I've found myself a bride," Gus laughed.

"Whom were you talking to?"

"Old friends," Gus boasted. "He is Judge Worth, and Nellie is his daughter. She has a brother who's studying to be a doctor."

"A judge for a father and a doctor for a brother. A girl like that must be pretty spoiled," Elisha scoffed.

"Nellie spoiled? I don't think so."

Elisha headed for the street. "A girl like that has everything going for her."

"Like what?"

"Family, education, money, clothes . . ." Elisha felt depressed. "It's been my experience that girls like that can be greedy."

"I know what you're thinking, Brooks: Frisco girls marry moneybags. Nellie may be headstrong, but she isn't greedy."

"You may find out different," Elisha warned.

Gus looked smug. "I may find out tonight."

"What's tonight?"

"Guess!" Gus teased.

Elisha looked his roommate over. Gus made a dashing figure in his English sport suit with shawl collar and pockets. His tweed suit was stitched around the edges in the latest style. His straw hat boasted the new low crown that seemed to be the rage among young fellows these days. Leather gaiters fastened with metal clips covered Gus's trousers to the knees. Bushy cheek whiskers gave him an extra dose of dash. Yes, a girl might fall for a fellow like Gus, Elisha mused. Gus knew how to approach girls.

"Guess what's tonight," Gus prompted.

Elisha didn't feel like guessing. "Don't play games with me."

"The Worths invited me for supper," Gus boasted. "They wanted you to come too, but I said that you'd rather memorize the dictionary."

76

"You said that?"

"It's true, isn't it? I saved you the trouble of having to say no."

"I suppose I should thank you," Elisha remarked. "Does the Judge know you're after his daughter?"

"I hope not," Gus laughed. "Judge Worth is known to turn suitors away."

"Why did he invite you?"

"He didn't. Nellie invited me, and he couldn't say no. You see, we were neighbors at Martinez in Contra Costa County."

"Neighbors?" Elisha felt sad. He thought of his childhood neighbors in faraway Michigan.

"My parents and the Worths lived in houses overlooking Carquines Strait," Gus explained. "Judge Worth was the county judge until his appointment to U.S. Deputy Marshal, a career advancement which required him to move to San Francisco."

"So you knew Nellie as a child."

Gus put on his smug smile. "We played in the Judge's garden. You should have seen his flowers! We picked the prettiest blossoms for Mrs. Worth, and she gave us warm cookies. We used to swing from the old oak trees and had lots of fun."

Elisha's mouth puckered. Swinging from trees and having fun with friends was not part of his childhood. He said, "Let's not talk about Nellie anymore."

Gus gave Elisha a sidelong glance. "What's eating you, Brooks?"

"Let's not talk about Nellie anymore," Elisha repeated.

That evening Gus took special pains getting ready and left for his dinner appointment with a swagger. Elisha waited up for him, and when he returned, he was displaying his smug smile.

Monday morning at the Mint a gentleman stopped by toward Elisha's desk. "Are you Mr. Brooks?" he asked.

"Yes, sir. What can I do for you?"

"I am the principal of the Urban Academy." The visitor spoke with pride. "I have been told that you hold a teacher's certificate. Is this correct, sir?"

Elisha pointed to a chair. "I've been issued a teacher's certificate, and I taught two eight-month terms in the gold country."

The principal sat down. "Experienced teachers are difficult to find. Would you consider teaching at my academy? It has come to my attention that your conduct is such as to be appropriate for a private academy."

Elisha resisted his urge to empty his desk drawers. A teaching position! Standing in a classroom, being entrusted with pupils, what more could he want?

The principal gave Elisha no time for contemplation. "Are you considering my offer, Mr. Brooks?"

"Yes, sir. Thank you for the offer and your confidence in me."

"Then you will come to Urban Academy?"

Elisha hesitated. Through the partially open door, he saw his benefactor poring over a report Elisha had prepared. Had it not been for Mr. Cheeseman, he might still be begging for odd jobs. Mr. Cheeseman valued his services, often commending him for his loyalty and zeal.

"In all fairness to Mr. Cheeseman, I must decline your offer, sir."

The principal coughed politely behind his hand. "We have not as yet discussed salary, sir. I can offer more pay than you are receiving at present."

Elisha needed money to buy a certain home site on Sutter street. A place of his own would give him privacy and independence. But he put brakes on himself. "It's not the money, sir. I do want to teach. However, I mustn't abandon my post here. It wouldn't be right."

"Will consider my offer later?"

"Perhaps."

The principal left and Elisha pounded his desk. Had he

blown the opportunity of a lifetime? A teaching position at a city academy might not come his way again. In his third year at the Mint, he was still doing a clerk's job. This was 1868. He was 27 years old, and he was failing the hopes of his mother. None of his brothers seemed bent on a teaching career, not even Elijah.

On the Sabbath, Elisha slicked back his hair and brushed his coat with extra care. He spotted Nellie's kneeling figure among the parishioners up front. Dust specks danced and shimmered around her in a shaft of spring sunlight. Her blond hair gleamed inside an attractive bonnet. Its streamers fell over the velvety bodice she wore over a crisp, white blouse. The Judge's daughter made a compelling picture. She wore quality clothes and looked like opportunity personified.

You're stupid, he scolded himself. *Keep away from girls and stay out of trouble.*

As he was leaving after the services, he felt Gus's hand on his shoulder. "I'll be a while, Brooks. Go home without me if you like. I want to talk with Nellie."

"I'll wait." Elisha let Gus stand in the pew to catch the girl. Once outside, he steered clear of the throng of people leaving the church. But to his surprise, Gus soon wound his way between the parishioners. Judging by his crestfallen look, something had gone wrong.

"Nellie wants to meet you, Brooks."

"Me?" Elisha wished he had left.

"I couldn't say no." Gus grabbed the bristling Elisha and dragged him over to the blond girl and her father.

"This is my roommate—"

Elisha suffered through the introduction. Why was Nellie smiling at him? Was she setting him up for mischief? Was she making fun of him? He felt gooseflesh under the scrutiny of her forthright blue eyes.

Judge Worth studied him with the same piercing blue eyes. "Why is it, young man, that you refuse to come over with Gus?" the judge demanded.

Elisha wasn't prepared for the judge's bluntness. The question made him feel hot and cold all at once. "F-for supper?" he stuttered.

Nellie sounded her musical laugh. "Please, do come over and have supper with us."

Elisha took in her rosy face, the blond locks, the innocent smile. In a flash, he recalled Rosie, the girl he had favored with wildflowers at Healdsburg. His face flushed as he recalled being booted down the porch steps in his $15 coat and suffering a bruised face.

"I'm sorry," he said. "I have important things to do."

The girl's face fell. She quickly joined her father when he said, "Let's go, Ellen."

Elisha hurried off. Once out of sight, he stopped and wiped his perspiring forehead. Gus hastened after him and proceeded to give him a tongue lashing.

"What's the matter with you, Brooks? Are you sick? Do you have a fever? I've never seen you behave like this."

"I'm sorry, Gus, but this girl gets to me."

"You made her feel terrible, Brooks. She must think you don't like her."

"I don't like her," Elisha countered. "I'd rather read than sit at her stuffy table."

"You stick to your books, Brooks. I'll go for the girl."

"Why, did she invite you again?"

"Not this time, thanks to you."

"I told you I'm sorry."

"You made a terrible impression," Gus scolded. "I don't think the Worths' will ever have anything to do with you again."

"I am sorry, Gus. How many times do you want me to apologize?" Elisha's plan for a quiet evening of reading was looking better all the time.

Chapter Eleven
Invitation to Tea

Elisha recognized the girl's slender figure, even from across the street. He ducked into a doorway, but she had already seen him.

"Mr. Brooks!" Nellie called above the traffic noise. Then to his dismay, she crossed the street without the slightest hesitation. "Are you hiding from me?" she asked. "You really shouldn't be so shy, you know."

Elisha stammered an excuse, but her cheeks flamed as she pinned her blue eyes on him. "We haven't seen Gus lately. Do you know what happened to him?"

"He moved out," Elisha explained. "He attends church in his new neighborhood, I suppose."

"I'm not surprised, and good riddance."

Elisha's eyes opened wide. "I thought Gus was your friend."

"He was a childhood companion, but he has changed."

"He has?"

"He thinks too much of himself! I told Gus that a fellow who cannot persuade his roommate to accept a supper invitation isn't much of a friend." She laughed her musical laugh. "Gus expects a girl to swoon over him, but he dreads competition."

"Y-you didn't swoon over him?"

"Over that conceited oaf?" Golden ringlets escaped the ribbon wreath she wore in her hair.

"Why did you want me over for supper?" Elisha asked.

"Didn't Gus tell you?"

"Tell me what?"

"That I like you?"

Elisha bristled. "Are you making fun of me? Surely you know that I'm a poor boy. I have no mansion, carriage, or family to boast about. I am not much of a catch."

She laughed. "That's just what I like about you, Elisha. You don't run after girls and make promises. You're honest—and modest to boot."

"You don't understand," Elisha said earnestly. "My father lost two business enterprises due to unforeseen events. He is an invalid on crutches. My mother died. My brothers barely make a living, and my youngest brothers live with merciful neighbors. As for myself, I sold wildflowers and did odd jobs to support myself while attending grammar school when I was 17 and 18. I worked as a janitor at Healdsburg Academy to pay for tuition." A lump pushed into his throat. "When I was thrown into the streets of San Francisco, I was destitute."

Nellie heard him out. "We must talk more about your life," she decided when he finished. "I want to learn everything about you. Can you come over for afternoon tea? I told Mother about you, and she wants to meet you."

Elisha felt cornered. "If I can get away," he hedged.

"Let's go now," Nellie urged.

"Now?" He smiled at her urgency; he couldn't help it.

She beamed up at him. "That's better, Elisha. For once that sad, sad look is gone from your eyes."

"Perhaps some other time," he said.

"Here." She pushed a slip of paper into his sweaty hand, then turned and disappeared in the street traffic.

The paper slip showed a scribbled Van Ness Street address. Elisha stuck it into his pocket. On his way back to the Mint, he grappled with mixed emotions. "A Judge's daughter, sister of a doctor," he muttered, "Hopeless from the start." Why couldn't she be a clerk's daughter, somebody with a modest background? Why couldn't they be more evenly matched? Why should a girl like Ellen Worth care for him? Why?

A surprise visitor awaited Elisha at his place of work. The land speculator who owned the lot on Sutter street greeted him with impatience. Elisha asked him to pull up a chair.

"I don't quite have the full amount for the site," he explained. "Can you give me another month?"

"That's why I'm here." The speculator's chair scraped on the floor as he leaned forward. "I need to sell now."

Elisha gulped. "I hate to lose the site. I'm already drawing up plans for the house."

"I need money for another deal right now," the speculator pressed. "Bring your cash tomorrow morning, and I'll have the papers drawn up."

"Are you selling me the site at a reduced price?"

"Yes, yes, just get the money."

Elisha couldn't believe his luck. The transaction was settled the next day, and he could call himself the proud owner of a piece of San Francisco!

What about Nellie? he asked himself after church the next Sabbath. Judge Worth gave him a cold shoulder, but Nellie brushed past Elisha while her father engaged himself in a conversation with other gentlemen. "Mother expects you for tea on Monday at 4:00. Can you come?" she whispered.

Elisha nodded.

Monday, at 4:00 sharp, he knocked on the door of a fine house on Van Ness. He felt apprehensive, half expecting to be thrown down the porch steps at any moment. Remembering his experience with Rosie, he didn't bring flowers this time.

A pleasant woman, wearing an ample skirt, answered the door. "Why, you must be Elisha Brooks, the young man my daughter has been talking about."

Elisha felt tongue-tied.

Mrs. Worth spoke in a friendly, motherly way, but her smiling face showed signs of sadness. "Nellie's description of you is correct," Mrs. Worth continued. "Tall, dark, and handsome indeed!" She took his hat and ushered him into the parlor. "Nellie, our guest is here!" she called. She winked at Elisha. "She's making herself extra pretty for you."

Elisha sat on the edge of the plush sofa. The Worths' parlor was fancier than anything he had seen in his life. Light streamed through a large bay window hung with fancy drapes, illuminating papered walls, exquisite lamps, houseplants, and a fireplace with bric-a-brac on the mantle. A large wing chair decorated with doilies seemed to be reserved for the man of the house.

Then Nellie entered with a tray. She placed a cup and saucer on a small table beside Elisha and poured fragrant tea from a porcelain pot. "Sugar?" she asked.

He nodded. Could this be happening to him? He barely raised his eyes to Nellie's white linen blouse and the ruffles at her throat. When she sat down beside him, he noticed that her hair was pulled away from her pretty face. As she turned, he saw that braids and loose curls trailed down her back. Between sips of soothing tea, he watched her fingers brush back escaping ringlets.

Mrs. Worth led the conversation with non-threatening questions. Warmed by her motherly interest, Elisha finally found his tongue. He spoke of his childhood on the Michigan farm and the westward trek in the covered wagon.

"You see, my father was already in California, that's why my brother and I did the driving," he concluded.

Mrs. Worth looked aghast. "Nellie's father also went ahead to California, but he came back to Nantucket Island

and put his family on a ship. We arrived here in 1852, when Nellie was 8."

"We also arrived in 1852!" Elisha exclaimed. "We settled at Bidwell Bar."

"We settled at Martinez," Mrs. Worth said. "We came to San Francisco in 1862."

"And I came to live in this city in 1865," Elisha said.

"What are your future plans, Elisha? Will you remain at the Mint?" Mrs. Worth asked.

Elisha squirmed. "I prepared for the career of teaching."

Nellie had been quiet for some time. Now she spoke up. "If teaching is your chosen profession, you should pursue it, Elisha."

He was afraid she'd say something brash like that. "For now, I'll stay at the Mint," he determined. "I owe it to my boss. Mr. Cheeseman relies on me."

"Mr. Cheeseman is an obstacle, Elisha. Obstacles can be overcome," Nellie said firmly.

"Nellie, you mustn't tell people what to do," her mother admonished.

Nellie smiled brightly. "May I tell Elisha to come for tea tomorrow?"

Her mother sighed.

Elisha hadn't noticed how time had flown. He rose. The sun no longer shone on the rug under his feet. "I'm afraid I overstayed," he apologized.

"Will you come back tomorrow?" Nellie sounded anxious.

He glanced at her mother, who smiled benevolently. "Please do us the honor, Elisha. We find your stories fascinating."

"Thank you, Mrs. Worth. You're very kind."

Nellie handed him his hat. She appeared overjoyed. "Mother likes you," she confided.

Chapter Twelve
Judge Worth

The next day Nellie answered Elisha's knock and took his hat. "Please have a seat, Elisha. I'll get tea." She was wearing the white linen blouse he liked.

"Where is Mrs. Worth?" he asked.

"Mother is unwell at the moment. She may join us later." Nellie disappeared into the kitchen. She returned with a tray and poured fragrant tea into two delicate cups.

Tongue-tied once more, Elisha lifted his cup to his lips. He had looked forward to the older woman's comforting presence. "I hope it isn't anything serious," he said.

"No, not really. My brother says it's nothing clinical. He says occasional depressive moods are normal in people who have suffered losses in their lives."

Losses? Not wanting to appear curious, he remained silent, sipping his tea, being careful not to break the fragile cup.

"Do you think it's normal for a person to be depressed, Elisha?"

"If your mother has lost a loved one, I can understand how she feels."

Nellie set down her cup. "Poor Elisha, you lost your dear mother."

"And my sister."

Nellie looked stunned."You had a sister who died?"

Elisha swallowed. "Vienna and I were close. She was two years older than I, and the best sister anybody ever had. She attended academy and graduated at the head of her class."

"Did she suffer an accident?"

"Not an accident. She married the man she loved and gave him a baby boy." Elisha suppressed a sob. "She died of childbed fever, Nellie. She was only 21."

"How dreadful!" Nellie rubbed Elisha's cold hand. Her blue eyes expressed true sorrow. "I too have lost sisters and brothers, Elisha. I understand your pain."

He pressed her hand against his face. "No wonder your mother is depressed, Nellie. Losing children is more than a mother can bear."

"Losing your mother and sister is more than a boy can bear, Elisha."

"Mother was the finest pioneer woman in all the West, Nellie, a true heroine."

"I am truly sorry, Elisha. Let me help you ease your pain."

Elisha let go of her hand. He wiped his cheeks, ashamed of his outburst. "What are you saying?"

"I want to be your wife, Elisha. You're a good man. People like and respect you. You're unlike the others."

"I am poor, Nellie. I have nothing more than a home site on Sutter street and a modest income at the Mint."

"No matter, Elisha. I know that some day people will pay you what you're worth."

Elisha's chest heaved. "What about your father?"

She traced his eyebrows. "Obstacles can be overcome, dear Elisha. We must think of something. Surely, you and Dad have things in common?"

"What does he like?"

"Flowers. Do you like flowers?"

Elisha brightened. "Flowers kept me in food back in

Oroville days. I dried some flowers and made a collection. If you ever visit the Academy of Sciences you'll see my Butte County flora exhibit at the herbarium."

He suddenly fell silent. The front door opened and Judge Worth entered. When he saw Elisha, his face turned an angry red. "Sir, what are you doing here in the company of my daughter?" he barked.

Elisha sprang up. "I, uh—"

"Please leave this house at once, and stay away from Ellen in the future."

Elisha hastily prepared to leave. Glancing sideways, he saw that Nellie's face also had turned red. "Dad, Mother invited Mr. Brooks!" she said in a controlled voice.

"Where is your mother?" the Judge asked stiffly.

"In her room. She's unwell at the moment."

"You ought to have told your mother's guest as much and sent him away."

Nellie drew in a deep breath. "I did not want to send him away, Dad."

"Why not? You know the rules."

"I am not a child anymore, Dad. I'll be 24 in June. Most girls my age are married and have their own house rules," Nellie said evenly.

"You are a child as long as you live in your parents' house. Remember that, Ellen!"

"If I obey childhood rules any longer, I'll be an old maid, Dad. Ever since we came to San Francisco, you have discouraged suitors who came calling for me. I will not turn this one away, Dad! Elisha Brooks is special, and I'll be proud to be his wife."

The Judge whirled on his daughter in shock. "Ellen, watch your tongue!"

"It's true, Dad. I'll be his wife, if he will have me."

Judge Worth looked at Elisha who stood, hat in hand, ready to leave. "Well, sir?" the judge challenged.

Elisha turned, opened the door, and let himself out.

The next Sabbath he slipped into the church with the latecomers and left before the Worths, who always sat up front.

Sunday dawned warm and glorious, so Elisha donned his old Union uniform and, pick and shovel on his shoulder, headed for his lot between Laguna and Buchanan. He had figured out all the details for the wooden cottage he was going to build. He'd buy the materials little by little without going into debt. By doing most of the work himself, he'd save money.

He labored with pick and shovel, digging out the basement he wanted for his workshop. He was shoveling dirt with gusto, preparing for the stone masons to take over, when the noon sun became oppressive. So he thrust the shovel into a dirt pile and devoured the sandwich and apple he had brought along. Then, sweaty and soiled, he took off his coat and continued to work.

Pausing to wipe his brow, he noticed a couple strolling up Sutter Street. The gentleman walked with a slight limp. The lady wore a full, blue skirt and a silky bolero jacket that opened at the front, exposing a white, pleated blouse. A jaunty bonnet tipped forward, shading her face.

Elisha turned his back to the street, expecting the elegant couple would pass on by. Shoveling with vigor, he forgot about the pedestrians until he heard a familiar voice behind him.

"What a nice place for a home, Dad! Let's stop and watch." Nellie's musical laugh rang out.

Elisha froze. He was filthy, and he smelled.

Nellie pretended not to notice Elisha's predicament. "Dad and I visited the Academy of Sciences!" she bubbled. "Why didn't you tell us that you are the institution's treasurer, Elisha?"

Elisha rubbed dirt from his hands and turned to face Judge Worth. "Did you like my flowers, sir?"

The judge cleared his throat. "Real nice, young man."

"That isn't what you said earlier, Dad. You used the word 'impressive,'" Nellie corrected.

"So I did." The judge's quizzical eyes appraised Elisha's digging. He shook his head. "I think you want to angle your house this way." He grasped the shovel and made markings on the ground.

"What's wrong with the way I planned it?" Elisha wiped his shirt sleeve across his perspiring forehead.

"Well, let's see . . ." Then the judge explained in detail where and when the sun rose and set during the different seasons.

Elisha listened carefully. "I know that you are knowledgeable about many things, sir. I plan to put the kitchen on the uphill side and—"

"No, no, Elisha!" Nellie interrupted. "The kitchen must be in back, and there must be a balcony."

"A balcony?" Elisha hadn't thought of that.

"People should be able to have breakfast or read outside. And if there are children"—she paused, blushing—"they can play outside without the mother worrying about their safety."

Elisha's head spun. "I plan to put the parlor facing downhill and my study up front." He demonstrated the locations with sweeping motions of his arm.

"No, Elisha, the parlor belongs up front," Nellie decided. "Visitors enter from the street and see the parlor first."

By the time Nellie and Judge Worth left, Elisha's head was buzzing like a beehive. He took up his pick and shovel and marched home. He'd need to rethink the entire structure and start all over from scratch. Judge Worth was right. Nellie was right. He had planned his house for a bachelor's convenience. And the way things looked, he wasn't going to remain a bachelor.

In the solitude of his room, Elisha drew up a new plan. He'd show it to Nellie and Judge Worth, provided he received another invitation.

Chapter Thirteen
Earthquake!

A hum of voices filled the churchyard after the services. Nellie was talking to an older lady, and her father was just leaving a group of men. Elisha approached the judge with some misgivings. "I have redrawn the plans for my house, sir. You gave me excellent ideas. The house did stand at an awkward angle—I had it all wrong."

The judge's bushy eyebrows lifted. He appeared pleased. "When can I look at the plans?"

"I can take them to the site," Elisha suggested. "Perhaps you have other ideas I might use."

A grin widened the judge's florid face. "Why not drop in at my house tomorrow afternoon?"

"Thank you, sir, I'll be there."

The next day, Judge Worth answered the door. Elisha looked around the parlor, hoping to see Nellie and Mrs. Worth.

"The women went out," Judge Worth said. "Let's go in back where we can spread out your plans." He led the way to a dazzling workshop. Tools of every size and description, meticulously arranged, lined the walls. Fine pieces of hardwood awaited the skilled hands of a craftsman. A large table commanded the center of the room.

Elisha hadn't expected anything so exciting. "I had no idea you work with tools, sir."

The judge pointed to the table. "I used to be a furniture and cabinet maker. I served seven years as an apprentice on Nantucket Island and learned my trade from the ground up."

"Then you changed your career . . ." Elisha said, unrolling his plans.

The judge nodded. "I left my trade for editorial work." I ran the *Islander,* a Nantucket newspaper."

"Then you changed your profession *again!*" Elisha spread out his plans.

"I certainly did. In 1845 I visited Washington, D.C., with letters of recommendation to President Polk requesting my appointment as Postmaster at Nantucket. I was granted an interview with President Polk, during which he asked detailed questions about the flourishing whaling industry at Nantucket."

"An interview at the White House!" Elisha gasped. "Did you get the appointment?"

"Yes, I did. I held the position of postmaster for four years, during which a disastrous fire destroyed the town's business section." The judge smiled. "The post office burned down, but the mail was saved."

"No doubt owing to your speedy and courageous action." Elisha weighed down the corners of his plans with wooden blocks that were stacked at the edge of the table. "How did you become a judge?"

"It's a long story, Elisha. I purchased the ship, *Fanny* of Sag Harbor, and boarded her on August 20, 1849, with other islanders. We arrived at San Francisco on February 21, 1850, and headed straight for the gold mines."

"With success, I suppose?"

"Oh, yes, I was lucky." Judge Worth's index finger traced Elisha's plans, pausing here, and pausing there. "I returned to Nantucket and brought my family back. We settled in Contra Costa County, where I studied law with

Marshal S. Chase. I received an appointment as notary public, was elected justice of the peace, became associate judge with Judge R. N. Wood, and then was appointed County Judge."

"Sir, I stand in awe of you." Why was Judge Worth telling him all this, Elisha wondered. He felt depressed. Perhaps Nellie's father was letting him know that an illustrious man like Judge Worth would never allow his daughter to marry an undistinguished man. To Elisha's distress, the Judge wasn't finished with his résumé.

"I was appointed United States Deputy Marshal in 1862 and moved my family to San Francisco. Yes, the United States Circuit Court has become my second home."

During his entire talk, Judge Worth hadn't missed a detail on Elisha's plans. "This corner needs improving," he pointed out. "This window must be enlarged . . . A door should lead from this room to that."

Elisha felt sick. Why bother changing anything? What

Blue-Eyed Grasses
Sisyrinchium

was the use? Why not build the bachelor's quarters he had planned from the beginning? "Thank you for your time and consideration, sir. I'll think about the alterations." Elisha rolled up his plans and marched straight to his building site. *A door here? A larger window there? A corner which needed improvement?* He'd have to sleep on it. *Why had Nellie been absent?* he fretted to himself. *Had she given up hope?*

Elisha concentrated on his construction project. With fall arriving and winter rains threatening, he had better get the foundation in place. After some deliberation, he made the changes suggested by Judge Worth.

Then on the morning of Wednesday, October 21, 1868, Elisha was rudely shaken from his sleep. The whole house rocked and shook. Doors and windows rattled. The kerosene lamp danced on the table. Drawers fell open and objects toppled from shelves. *Earthquake!* Jolted out of bed, he felt alarm, fear, terror. His bedstead was moving; the room shuddered. And still the roaring, rocking, shaking, and rattling continued.

He thought of Nellie. He must hurry to her house. Perhaps she needed help. On the other hand, he was late for the office. When the shaking stopped, he pulled on his clothing. His toolbox, containing his hammer, saw, and chisels, had been slammed against a wall. He grabbed it and headed for the Mint.

The city presented a dizzying sight. Ruin and chaos was everywhere—fallen walls, collapsed chimneys, twisted horsecar tracks. People headed for their work places in a state of shock.

Mr. Cheeseman greeted Elisha at the door. "Thank God, you're here!" he cried. "Thank God, you have tools. It may be days until we can get tradesmen in to fix things."

The office was a shambles. There were books piled on the floor, lamps shaken down, pictures dangling at crazy angles, inkwells spilled. Mr. Cheeseman's desk had wandered into a corner and a window was broken, admitting cold air.

Elisha spent hours fastening shelves and returning things to their proper places. He was rearranging the jumbled pages of a report when someone pushed the door open. Nellie rushed into the room and threw her arms around Elisha's neck.

"Dear Elisha, thank God you are safe!"

He grasped her tiny waist. She was trembling. "You ought to stay in the safety of your house," he scolded.

"Safety!" she exclaimed. "There's no safety anywhere. I was worried sick about you. It took me forever to get here. Public transportation is at a standstill. You can't even get a cab. People say we may experience aftershocks. They say buildings on filled ground along the waterfront sustained the worst damage. I saw houses that slipped off their foundations and brick buildings that fell apart." She tried to calm herself before going on.

"Fortunately, the earthquake struck before schools were in session. Children and teachers could have been killed. Even so, we'll be hearing of casualties. It's too early to know the extent of the damage."

"You braved all this to find me!" Elisha marveled. He had expected to see a hysterical girl, one who cried and carried on.

"We must never part again, dear Elisha! I couldn't bear to have us separated when the next one strikes."

"I believe your father wants to keep us apart."

"Father's resistance is an obstacle we must overcome," she said firmly. "Do you have any ancestors worth mentioning?"

"Do I have *what?*"

She laughed her charming little laugh. "Dad believes in blood lines. You see, our roots go back to the *Mayflower* and, before that, to England."

Elisha recalled things Mother had told him in the Michigan cabin and on the wagon train. He smiled. "Perhaps my ancestors *will* impress Judge Worth."

"That would be a start," Nellie beamed. "Tell me about them so I can relay the information to Dad at an opportune moment."

While aftershocks made the earth shudder, Elisha tried to remember details. He found an apple in the top drawer of his desk and shared it with Nellie for their lunch.

"First, the Brookses, and then the Scholfields," he began. "You mentioned England. There is a tradition in my family that three Brooks brothers came over from Yorkshire a few years after the *Mayflower,* and that one of their descendants fought in the Revolutionary War. The records show that this old Continental was my great grandfather."

"What about the Scholfields?" Nellie asked.

"On my mother's side, the Scholfields were woolen manufacturers in England. Hoping to make their fortune, two brothers hid themselves aboard a ship bound for America." Elisha smiled at Nellie's eager attention. "In those days no skilled artisan was allowed to leave England, and neither machinery nor plans were allowed to leave the country. But these two Scholfield brothers carried their plans and know-how in their heads.

"On arrival in Connecticut, they built a mill with the necessary machinery, however, no one would buy their cloth. One day a merchant asked one of the brothers to look at some fine broadcloth he had just imported from England. Scholfield looked it over and . . ."

"And what?" Nellie's blue eyes were fastened on Elisha.

"Scholfield showed that the trademark on the cloth was his own."

"Then what happened?"

"The Scholfields' cloth sold after that, and President Madison was inaugurated in a suit of broadcloth presented to him by the brothers." Elisha cleared his throat. "The grandson of one of these two Scholfield brothers was my grandfather." He paused, letting the information sink in. "Do you suppose any of this will impress your father?"

"Oh, I think so," Nellie assured him, getting up. "I must get back. Father is due in court and I mustn't leave Mother alone."

"I'll escort you," Elisha offered.

"No, I can manage." She was out the door before Elisha could reach for his coat.

Elisha shook his head. What a girl!

Chapter Fourteen
A Wedding

Elisha studied the November sky. Gray clouds obscured the sun. *How long until the rains begin?* he wondered. *I must hurry to get the frame up,* he told himself. *Once the roof is on, I can work inside.* He fastened the mudsill to the foundation the stone masons had built prior to the earthquake.

He wanted to leave the city and its shaking ground, but what would become of Nellie if he did? He couldn't bear the thought that somebody like Gus might carry her off.

The earthquake had taught him how to build a stronger house. His wooden structure must not slip off the foundation. No stones must fall apart. God willing, his house would stand. He was working with his usual vigor when he saw Judge Worth limping toward him.

"I see you can use a hand, Elisha," the judge called out.

Elisha straightened up. "Do you know a qualified person who will work for reasonable wages?"

"Indeed I do, and this one works for free!" The judge pulled a ruler from his baggy pants and started to measure the southwest corner. He nodded with obvious satisfaction. "I see you improved the corner. Smart move."

"I warn you, sir, construction is hard work." Elisha wondered what advice the Judge would dole out next.

"Nellie told me about your ancestors." The judge picked up Elisha's saw, measured a board, then made a precise angle cut.

Elisha frowned. "I'm certain my ancestors are modest people compared to yours, sir."

"Oh, but they are impressive." Judge Worth appraised the cut he had made with critical eyes. "Ellen tells me that you are anxious to learn about her heritage."

"She is very proud of her ancestors." Elisha kept on working; time was of the essence if he was to finish his house before winter.

"She is a descendant of the Pilgrim fathers, who landed at Plymouth on December 22, 1620, and of the early settlers of Nantucket," the Judge explained.

Had Judge Worth come to help or to talk? Elisha wondered.

"My wife, Mary Elkins, was a daughter of Joseph Mayo, whose father was Joseph, son of John, son of Reverend John Mayo," the Judge continued.

Elisha wiped a sleeve over his forehead. He felt himself shrink with each illustrious name he heard. Now the judge began to recite from the Domesday Book.

"The family of de la Worth, afterward called Worth, came from Normandy with William the Conqueror in his invasion into England in 1066—Are you paying attention, Elisha?" the judge interrupted himself.

Elisha looked up. "Oh, yes, sir!"

"As I was saying," the judge continued, "the name Worth deserves respect; it must never be taken for granted by any descendant, no matter how far removed."

Elisha troweled cement before it set up. "I'm certain your daughter will teach her children respect for her maiden name, sir. The name Worth will also be held in high honor by your future son-in-law."

The judge brushed sawdust from his pants, then stuck the ruler back into his pocket. "I am expected for tea," he said abruptly.

"Thank you for helping," Elisha said. "Your ancestors are fascinating people."

"Are you doing anything special for Thanksgiving?" the judge asked.

Elisha shook his head.

"In that case, Mrs. Worth and I should be glad to have you over for dinner."

"Thank you, sir." He noticed the judge hadn't mentioned Nellie.

Thanksgiving dinner, served in the Worths' dining room, was the most sumptuous meal Elisha remembered. The cozy house was filled with enticing aromas. When dinner was over, Nellie and her mother cleared the table, and the Judge ushered Elisha into the parlor. Elisha took his place on the sofa. The Judge added a log to the fire, then settled himself in his wing chair.

Then, without preamble, he asked, "What is your opinion of my daughter Ellen?"

"I think she is a very remarkable girl, sir. Like you in many ways."

The judge frowned. "How so?"

"She is composed and in control, not a subordinate type. Despite her illustrious family, she is natural and unaffected." Elisha stopped, wondering if he had said too much.

"What else can you tell me about Ellen?"

Gus, Elisha's former roommate, came to mind. "Hers is an ability to estimate human nature, sir. She is not easily duped. She has horse sense."

"Are you comparing my daughter to a horse?"

"No, of course not!" Only then did Elisha detect the twinkle in the older man's bright blue eyes. "She takes her looks and mannerisms from you, sir. Same blue eyes and liveliness. She'll have bouncy, bubbly, beautiful babies, I'm sure."

Judge Worth leaned back in his chair, resting his hands on the crocheted doilies covering the armrests. Then he popped another question. "And what are your intentions in regard to my daughter?"

Elisha swallowed. "To a clerk's daughter I'd have proposed months ago, sir. Nellie and I . . ."

Nellie flung open the kitchen door, cheeks flaming. "Did you talk about me, Dad?" she demanded.

Judge Worth nodded. "Our guest was about to tell me about himself and you."

Her blue eyes blazed at Elisha. "And what about you and me?"

"We, uh, ought to get married," Elisha blurted.

She set down the tray she was carrying and flew into her father's arms. "God bless you, Dad!"

"Now, now, this is no reason to fall apart," The judge chuckled, stroking her blond hair. Nellie's body shook as she sobbed without control. The judge looked past her to Elisha. "You see what you've started? This child hasn't been the same since she first saw you."

Mrs. Worth entered from the kitchen. "What's going on?"

"Oh, Mother, Elisha and I are engaged!" Nellie flung her arms around her mother, laughing and crying all at once.

"Is this true?" Mrs. Worth questioned Elisha.

He nodded, barely able to contain himself. God was giving him, a poor man, a lovely wife!

Nellie sat down beside Elisha while her mother poured tea into very ordinary cups. "The earthquake ruined our delicate china," she apologized.

"Now, what about the wedding?" Judge Worth prompted. "We must set a date. How about Christmas?"

"I must finish the house first," Elisha objected.

"I can help you in my free time," the judge offered, "and I will make the furniture to get you started. It will be my wedding present."

my wedding present."

"Nellie and I can make curtains and other embellishments," Mrs. Worth added.

"We also must sew my wedding dress," Nellie reminded her mother.

The Judge sat up straight. "The wedding must be a grand social affair, one becoming the name of Worth."

"A grand wedding after the earthquake? Is this wise, dear?" Mrs. Worth questioned. "Getting a large hall may be difficult. Many structures were damaged."

"Mother is right," Nellie agreed. "I wouldn't want any plaster or chandeliers to fall on our guests. I don't care about a grand social event. All I want is Elisha."

She turned to Elisha. "What about you? Do you expect a big wedding?"

"This is not for me to decide, Nellie. Perhaps a small wedding would be easier on your mother."

Judge Worth shook his head. "We must stage a wed-

Wild Lupine
Lupinus perennis

ding San Franciscans will remember. And you, Ellen, must wear a magnificent gown." He reached for a slice of pumpkin pie on the lamp table beside his chair.

"Oh, Dad, it's not the dress or trimmings that count! The important thing is that Elisha and I are joined in holy wedlock."

"In that case, why not make it a May wedding and hold the reception here?" Judge Worth said.

"Or how about a June wedding?" Mrs. Worth suggested.

Nellie objected. "I'can't wait that long, Mother. Let's make it April." Eyes sparkling, she turned to Elisha. "Can we move in by April?"

"I hope so, Nellie. I'll work every free minute to finish our cottage."

In the end, everybody agreed on April 20, 1869. The wedding was a small affair with only Mr. Cheeseman and family members attending. The Worths' house overflowed with flowers—lilies, tulips, ranunculus, rhododendrons, primulas, and camellias. The bride herself chose a dainty bouquet of fragrant lilies-of-the-valley.

Nellie looked lovely. The belted dress she and her mother had sewn conveyed a sense of motion, even while she stood at the altar. The skirt flared with modest fullness up the front and billowed charmingly in back. Lace adorned her throat, and long sleeves enveloped her slender arms.

Elisha couldn't look at her enough. He wanted to run his fingers through her hair and lift the wreath of blossoms crowning her head. He felt like undoing the braids and curls cascading over her back. Her blue eyes sparkled up at him. Her rosy cheeks reflected the excitement Elisha felt inside. *Had Vienna looked so pretty on her wedding day?* he wondered. *Had John, his sister's groom, felt so happy?*

He carried his bride over the threshold of their modest little cottage that still smelled of paint and wood stain. Arms around his neck, Nellie said, "This is our place, Elisha. We will be happy here."

Chapter Fifteen
The Teacher

Cooking odors welcomed Elisha at the door of his house. He hung up his hat and entered the kitchen. "Nellie, I'm home!" he called.

"Dear Elisha!" She turned from the stove, wiping her hands on the apron tied around her slim waist, and kissed him.

Weeks had passed since the wedding, and Elisha still couldn't believe his luck. Not since his childhood had somebody cooked for him and greeted him with a kiss.

Nellie turned to lift a steaming pot from the burner. She set it aside, then faced him and asked, "Is anything wrong, dear?"

Elisha marveled at her ability to read his mind. "Mr. Cheeseman is leaving, Nellie. A new man is taking his place, and he'll bring his own staff."

"When did you learn about this?"

"This afternoon."

"What did Mr. Cheeseman say?"

"He advised me to find a new position."

Nellie beamed her brightest smile. "Now is your chance to get back into teaching, Elisha. Is the position at Urban Academy still open?"

"The principal has come by several times, offering me a partnership."

"Go to him the first thing in the morning, Elisha. Tell him you accept his offer."

"You're so positive, Nellie," Elisha marveled.

"You underestimate yourself," she scolded him. "Mr. Cheeseman recognized your qualities. After all, he retained your services for three and a half years. The president of the Academy of Sciences sent a letter praising your excellent services as treasurer." She laughed. "Last, but not least, Dad gave you his precious Ellen for a wife!"

Elisha swung her around. "Your dad gave me the best present I ever got." He felt validated. Nellie was unlike his mother in looks and behavior, yet she was wonderful in her own right. Whenever he voiced a vexing problem, she took things in stride.

He brushed damp ringlets from her forehead. He was still almost afraid to touch her. At times he reminded himself that she was not fragile, like the tea cups in her mother's house. The cups broke during the earthquake; Nellie hadn't.

He smiled down at her. "I don't know how I managed without you. You're always in control. Nothing fazes you."

"What would I do without *you?*" she asked. "You were quite a challenge to me, Elisha. Many times I despaired of getting your attention. You were so shy. I never saw you courting a girl, yet when I smiled in your direction you looked away."

"I didn't mean to," Elisha apologized.

She hugged him. "I am so blessed—I have a handsome husband with moral character, one who's also very bright." She traced his eyebrows. "I love your lean, taut face."

He felt heat rising to his cheeks. "You embarrass me, Nellie."

She flicked a finger at his lapel. "For a man with your

looks and talent, you are too modest and too serious."

"And you are too independent," he teased.

"I do what I think is right."

"You're supposed to obey your husband," he said in mock seriousness.

She stood in front of him, laughing. "I'm not your slave, Elisha. You freed the slaves, remember?"

He kept a straight face. "I've never known a girl like you, Nellie. You have your own mind and you make your own decisions."

"My decisions are usually sound, aren't they?" Her blue eyes twinkled.

"Of course, they are," Elisha chuckled. She was teaching him that his mother had been the rarest jewel, but Nellie made him laugh.

He got the position at Urban Academy the next day. After leaving the Mint, he began to teach the children of wealthy parents. During the seven years he taught mathematics and English at the private academy, he observed misbehaving boys and girls on weekends and on his way home from school. Wasn't anybody teaching these children good conduct? Didn't children learn right from wrong anymore? Were there no teachers demonstrating the laws of God? Elisha asked himself troubling questions during quiet hours and when sleep eluded him at night.

Finally, his nagging conscience prompted him to pursue a public school appointment. He applied for a position that required letters of recommendation and a life diploma. Elisha presented letters of appreciation he had received from prominent citizens. When he handed over the stack, the clerk checked letterheads and signatures, then pulled out two letters. The first letter showed beautiful penmanship presented in purplish ink.

The clerk's eyes popped. "Why, it's from one of the 'Big Four' railroad barons who brought the transcontinental railroad to California!" he exclaimed. Then he read portions of the letter:

Mr. Elisha Brooks
My Dear Sir,

We regret to hear you have resigned your position as a teacher of the Urban Academy . . . Believing Timothy's satisfactory progress in his studies is in large degree due to your talent and tact as a teacher, Mrs. Hopkins and myself desire to express to you our thanks.

Teaching is a profession, or perhaps more strictly speaking, an art, in which the talent to acquire knowledge is essential, but the more rare talent and tact of imparting it is indispensable to success.

Hoping your services as a teacher are not to be hereafter lost to the youth of San Francisco, and wishing you personal success,

I am yours
Very respectfully,
Mark Hopkins

The clerk reached for the second letter. Written in haste by a busy businessman, it was signed by A.B. Forbes, General Agent for the Pacific Coast, Mutual Life Insurance Company of New York. Again, the clerk read excerpts.

Mr. Elisha Brooks,
Dear Sir,

It gives me pleasure to testify to your ability and faithfulness as a teacher. My two sons, now within second year in Yale College, were graduated from the Urban Academy in their Preparatory Course, partly under your tuition, and the thorough training they received there has been invaluable.

A grin spread over the clerk's face. "With letters like these, you can't possibly miss, provided you beat your competitors in the exam." Elisha did win out over his competitors and was offered the position of teacher and vice principal at the Washington Grammar School. He happily accepted.

"You'll be called upon to handle bad boys," teachers

warned. "Some bad boys may get back to you."

"Every boy has good qualities," Elisha stressed. Teachers had given up on certain youngsters, he feared. He was determined to develop the boys' best qualities and take his chances.

His talent to turn boys around soon became known. Other schools began transfering "incorrigibles" to Elisha's classroom.

"Someday you'll be sorry," teachers warned again. "Some students hold grudges."

"A teacher must give his best, no matter what," he replied.

Elisha taught by example. He gained the attention and respect of his charges by relating incidents from his boyhood. His westward trek, milk delivery in gold mining camps, and his struggle to put himself through grammar school as a teenager quieted even the most unruly boy.

Truancy dropped as students looked forward to attending Elisha's classes. They regarded this teacher, who had driven a team of oxen and a covered wagon across the country at the age of 11, with awe.

"He's tough," boys told one another at recess. "He's tough, but he respects us. Let's not cross him."

After three years at Washington Grammar, Elisha entered a competitive examination for the principalship of the Eighth Street Grammar School (soon renamed Franklin), in the city's roughest part. This school was one of the city's largest and the most difficult to manage. With 1,000 students, including 600 girls, and 18 teachers, a principal needed top qualifications.

On the day of the exam, Nellie met Elisha at the door of their home. "How did you manage, dear?"

Elisha felt drained. "It will be a while until I know the results." The exam had been demanding. He was glad to be home. "Where are the children, Nellie?"

She pointed to the balcony in back of the kitchen. "Fred

and Joe are building a dog house for a friend who got a puppy. I told the boys they could use your tools. It's all right, isn't it?"

Elisha nodded. His hand-made tools lined his basement workshop. The boys knew which tools they were allowed to use. "What are the girls doing?" he asked.

"Alice is doing her homework, and Mother is on the balcony bouncing Myrtle."

"She has been over a lot lately," Elisha remarked. He stuck his head out onto the balcony to greet his mother-in-law. "She looks happy," he told Nellie.

Nellie beamed. "Mother hasn't had a sick day since our babies came along. She adores our children."

Elisha marveled at his home life. He recounted his blessings daily. No longer was he a hungry, penniless boy. He had a family, a house, and a fine reputation as a teacher. He owned a piano for Alice to practice on, tools for the boys to learn with, and a balcony where his children played in safety with their playmates.

And there was Jay, his handsome young brother, whom he and Nellie had taken into their household. The children called him "Uncle Jay." He and Nellie had tried unsuccessfully to bring his other brothers and Vienna's young son to San Francisco. Elisha sighed. His family had scattered, and he had lost contact with his twin, Elijah.

One of his sons tore into the kitchen. "I need another saw, Mother."

"Hold it!" Elisha caught the boy on his way to the basement. "How many saws are you using?"

"Two."

"Two saws are enough, son."

The boy trudged back to the kitchen. "Dad is so strict, Mother. He's always right," he complained.

Nellie took the boy aside. "He is," she agreed. "He is, and you have a long way to go to be like him."

The boy squirmed, but Nellie continued her lecture.

"Your dad helped his family on the farm when he was your age, Joe. Later on, he supported his parents and worked to put himself through school. You can play with friends and look forward to a fine education. When people call you Dr. Brooks some day, remember that your dad made it possible."

"Oh, Mother!" the boy sighed, escaping to the balcony.

Elisha faced Nellie. "What do you make of that boy?"

Nellie laughed. "Boys test their power to see how far they can go. Boys will be boys."

Elisha withdrew to his study. He remembered the day his own mother drew him aside, saying, "You must respect your father, Elisha. It is the law of God." As he graded papers he listened to the cheerful tune Alice played on the piano in the parlor. Hammer blows from the boys' project sounded from the balcony.

Nellie raises happy children, Elisha told himself. *Alice, Fred, Joe, and Myrtle enjoy a mother's love and a grandmother's devotion.* He wondered what Grandmother Scholfield had been like. He wished he had known this fine woman. Sighing, he thought again how wonderful it would be if his own mother could visit the children and impart lessons only she could give! How wonderful if his sister Vienna could drop by!

Mrs. Worth was the only grandmother his children would ever know. His mother was dead, Vienna was dead, and his brothers were scattered. Elisha stopped grading papers. He himself had missed much, but his children were growing up in a stable family. "God has given me a family of my own," Elisha whispered. "God is restoring the years that the locusts have eaten."

Chapter Sixteen
Up the Ladder

Elisha sat comfortably in his straight-backed chair. The dining room was cozy this November day in 1879. Cooking odors drifted from the kitchen, children's laughter sounded from the balcony, and cable car noises on the new Sutter Street line made themselves heard.

Judge Worth faced Elisha across the table. "I hear you are making a success of the Eighth Street School. What changes have you made?"

"First of all," Elisha began, "I train teachers to aim for formation of character. Teachers must uplift students, and students must love coming to school."

"Love coming to school? How can this be accomplished?" Judge Worth raised his bushy eyebrows. At age 70, he was as lively as ever.

"I made some innovations," Elisha explained. "For example, we started a carpenter's shop. Students may stay after school and work with tools. They can take home the objects they make."

"Who teaches them, and who pays for that?"

"Sometimes I do, and sometimes teachers volunteer. We charge each student 25 cents per month."

"What else is new at your school?" Judge Worth asked.

"We have a literary club," Elisha informed his father-in-law. "Students may read the books we offer and recite poems. The club is free and very popular."

The judge nodded. "Reading is so important. Without the ability to read a person cannot progress."

Elisha agreed. "Before I learned how to read I was unable to pass a simple test. My boss told me I'd be a bark stripper for the rest of my life."

The judge stroked his silver beard. "I needed reading and writing at every step of my career. What other innovations have you made at the school?"

"We stress calisthenics, and we started a course in drawing."

"What about the basic subjects? Are your students learning those?"

"Oh, yes! Our students do honest work and fully master their subjects." Elisha hesitated. "If they fall behind, they're denied admission to the most popular classes."

Alice slid into her seat beside Elisha and laid her curly head on his arm. Elisha smiled at the 9-year-old. Alice, the firstborn, was crazy about her daddy.

Fred, the 7-year-old, followed his grandfather's beckoning. Judge Worth patted the boy's hand. "How are you, dear Frederick?"

"Fine, Grandpa." Fred was called by Judge Worth's middle name. The two were close.

Jay, Elisha's younger brother, and 5-year-old Joe entered the room together. Joe scrambled into his seat and Jay sat down beside him.

Nellie guided Myrtle to the table. "Sit in my chair, darling. You can sit on my lap later, all right?"

Myrtle's large, dark eyes looked up at Nellie. Elisha's heart melted. Myrtle was a sweet little girl. Her looks reminded him of Mother and Vienna.

Nellie made several trips to the kitchen, always returning with a heaped platter. She had tied a starched white apron over the black dress she had worn since her mother's sudden death a month earlier.

Judge Worth unfolded his napkin. "I had hoped Mary and I could retire in Martinez," he said. "Living in the house I built there was almost like living on Nantucket Island. The house commands a glorious view of the Straits of Carquinez."

"You can still go there, Dad," Nellie encouraged. "Someday Elisha will consider retirement, and we'll build a house next to yours."

Judge Worth speared a steaming potato from the platter she handed him. "Would you consider moving to Contra Costa county? Bright sunshine, fine flowers, plenty of water."

Elisha spooned sour cream on his baked potato and topped it with pungent chives. "Water has always instilled a certain fear in me, sir."

"Fear? Fear of water?" The judge's eyes grew big.

Nellie came to Elisha's rescue. "You cannot imagine the dreadful experiences Elisha had with water, Dad. Why, he almost lost his mother and little brother at a place called 'Slough of Despond' on their westward journey. Then his mother and her six children crossed the flooded Missouri on a raft and nearly drowned. In California a creek washed away his father's sawmill. Then the Feather River went on a rampage, stranding his family."

Judge Worth looked stunned. "It appears that water has been a villain in your life."

Elisha changed the subject. "How will you spend your time once you retire, sir?"

Judge Worth brightened. "Writing and researching the history of Nantucket families will keep me busy for years."

Nellie handed Elisha a basket filled with warm biscuits. "Where would you like to live, dear?" she asked. "I know you're not fond of the city, located as it is at the tip of a peninsula and surrounded by water."

Elisha buttered one of Nellie's featherlight biscuits and

put it aside. "I love trees, Nellie. Trees, hills, and a pleasant climate are to my liking."

"Where would you find your ideal location?" asked the judge.

"On camping trips with teachers and family I found wonderful places, sir. I am still looking for the perfect place, however."

In his first year as principal of the Eighth Street (Franklin) Grammar School, Elisha was eons away from retirement. The school between Harrison and Bryant kept him busy for a dozen years.

One morning, Elisha opened a letter dated May 28, 1891. He read it aloud.

Dear Sir:

At a meeting of the Board of Education, held on the 27th inst., you were transferred from your position as Principal of the Franklin Grammar School to the position of Principal of the Cogswell Mission High School.

So Elisha cleared out his desk and bid his students and teachers goodbye.

Another letter from the Secretary of the Board of Education reached Elisha a year later. He read the important document aloud.

Dear Sir:

At a meeting of the Board of Education, held on the 11th inst., you were elected to the position of Principal of the Girls' High School, your election to take effect July 1, 1892.

Elisha let out a loud "Whoopie!"

At the end of the school year, he once more cleared out his desk. Before tossing the newspaper into the waste basket, he read sections of the article his secretary had circled.

The principalship of the Girls' High School is a rare political plum . . . It is a life position with a salary of $250 a month, a commanding position and one coveted by every teacher with a high school certificate in the city. The salary *and position . . . are sufficient to attract eminent high school teachers. . . . Girls' High School is regarded as the highest and most desirable position in the state's public schools. This school demands refinement, justice, integrity, and its principal enjoys tremendous prestige. It is a position of power and influence.*

Could this be happening to him? Mother would be so proud. "I wish you were here," he whispered.

The new principal surprised everybody by forbidding physical punishment at Girls' High.

"Why not discipline the girls?" the teachers asked.

"I know that old proverb 'Spare the rod and spoil the child' must sometimes be applied when a boy gets mulish, but these girls are as far removed from mules as the North Star is from the Southern Cross," Elisha replied.

The morning of July 14, 1892, a reporter headed for Girls' High School at the corner of Scott and Geary streets. He jotted down his impressions as he studied the brand new building: *An immense and handsome structure. Four stories and a basement. Romanesque architecture. Pressed brick, handsomely turned with standstone and granite. Slate roof. Main entrance on Scott.* Then he took the wide flight of granite stairs leading to the front entrance, turned right, then knocked at the office of Principal Brooks.

"Come in!" Elisha invited.

The reporter introduced himself and started to ask questions. "Girls' High opened in June and is now fully occupied. Is this correct, sir?"

Elisha nodded. "We've got an excellent start and anticipate a pleasant and fruitful year. Let me show you around." He took the reporter through the spacious hall and explained special features. "The wood finish is very handsome, of natural wood, highly polished," he pointed out. "The doors are made of sugar pine. The wainscoating is of cedar. Fine craftsmanship indeed."

The reporter gasped at seeing the chemical laboratory

on the ground floor. He admired the library and reception room next to the Principal's office. He noted the teachers' rooms, closets, and cloakrooms, as well as the lunch and dressing rooms.

Elisha showed him the classrooms on all floors. Teachers smiled as Elisha introduced the visitor. Slim-waisted girls turned heads piled high with hair and giggled in embarrassment.

"How you can remember the names of your teachers is beyond me!" The reporter said, scribbling furiously in his notebook. He often had to ask Elisha to repeat the spelling of a name.

"I value my teachers," Elisha replied. Memorizing their names very quickly makes for a harmonious collaboration."

They were leaving Miss Fowler's Normal class in the south wing, where 80 pupils prepared themselves for a teaching career. At the top of the last flight of stairs, Elisha opened a huge door, chuckling in anticipation.

The reporter's gasped, his eyes wide. "What's this?"

"The attic," Elisha grinned, remembering his own first reaction to the gaping space. "The hall isn't finished yet, but it will be a grand place for concerts and public receptions." He pointed to the enormous stage in the background. "This is where our graduates will receive their diplomas. We have space for 200 chairs and can accomodate 2,500 people in all."

"You must be delighted with this wonderful school, sir!" The reporter stepped to an arched window. "What about the grounds?"

"We have plenty of space around the building. The men you see far below are putting in the lawns. I have future plans for a greenhouse and a botanical garden."

After the interview, Elisha spent a quiet moment in his office. He was in charge of this grand school. Teachers called him a self-made man. Self-made? He repeated a saying of his mother. "By God all things are possible."

Chapter Seventeen
Camping in the Redwoods

Elisha rested on a log at the base of a towering redwood. Wind rushed in branches that met the sky. Velvety leaves nodded in time to water that gurgled at his feet as it flowed over rocks and spilled into a crystal basin. Ferns dipped and waved. He filled his lungs with the woodsy air, inhaling deeply as he observed his peaceful surroundings.

All plants here seemed designed for giants. Huge clover leaves shared space with violet, heart-shaped leaves the size of saucers. Rough-barked tree trunks were large enough for a team and wagon to pass through. Among man-high feathery bushes, arm-long oval leaves, and house-high berry bushes, human problems seemed to recede.

A giant golden slug nestled in a mossy place, perhaps hiding from a screeching Steller blue jay. The saucy bird perched on a branch, watching Elisha, his black topknot standing up like the tiara of a monarch. Satisfied that the intruder meant no harm, the jay whirred through shrubbery, looking like a streak of blue velvet.

Elisha sighed. To own a nest in such a peaceful setting! What would it take to build a cabin in the redwoods? The turn of the century was approaching, demanding new directions. True peace eluded Elisha. In his mind loomed newspaper articles with lurid headlines and caricature drawings of himself. Months earlier, he had become the target of public ridicule. A reporter, who had found him digging the soil in the school's botanical garden, called him a "farmer." Dr. Drucker, the current director of the school board, and two self-serving teachers claimed that Elisha wasn't doing his job properly.

"They made me the butt of unfair accusations," Elisha muttered. "I always followed my conscience. I dealt fairly with everybody. I did what was good and right, as best I knew it." He sighed again. "Teachers warned me that some bad boy might one day get back at me. They were right. Drucker repaid me with hate."

Elisha got up and hiked on. He was a good distance ahead of his party of campers, for campers half his age were rarely able to keep up with him. A clearing came into view. Camp Brooks lay before him. The camp in Boulder Creek, south of San Francisco, was flecked with sunlight. Ten large tents containing redwood bedsteads, tables, camp stools, and canvas floors stood in a semicircle around an open slope crowned with graceful trees.

Nellie sat in her wicker chair outside a tent decorated with ferns and fragrant azaleas. She was reading and staying out of the sun. Her fair skin had a way of getting red as a cooked lobster. She saw him and pointed to the camp's "lovebirds".

Myrtle and her beau, a young businessman and Christian movement leader, sat on a blanket, bantering. Elisha smiled. Charles Milton Whitney was a man after his own heart. He winked at Nellie. It had been years since he and Nellie had felt that way. Their relationship had deepened and matured. Elisha knew he had been a lucky man to get that Nantucket girl for his wife. There wasn't another one like her.

He passed long tables and waved at the two pigtailed

Celestials who busied themselves at the camp kitchen. Cooking odors and sizzling sounds proved that the Chinese cooks would soon serve dinner. And after sunset, campers would gather around a great fire and relate the day's adventures. Then they'd all sing jolly camp songs to the accompaniment of a flutist.

Happy voices drifted up from the staircase cut into the hillside, leading down to the San Lorenzo creek at the bottom of the canyon. The stream was dammed up, allowing campers the pleasures of boating.

Elisha kissed Nellie's warm cheek. "How was your day?"

"Fine. How about yours?" Nellie's blue eyes studied him. "Is anything wrong, dear?"

Elisha drew up a campstool. "Every summer for 20 years we have taken family and teachers to Camp Brooks," he mused.

"These have been happy times, Elisha. After a month of camping, everybody returns to the city refreshed."

"I can't seem to get into the camping spirit this year," Elisha confessed.

"Why not? It's that Drucker thing, isn' it?"

"You always read my mind, Nellie." He looked up and waved to three teachers coming up the staircase.

"Here's the Captain of the Camp!" they called.

"Come join us." Elisha invited, and readied campstools for the two men and the lady.

Nellie winked at the teachers. "I believe our captain is still stewing over Drucker."

"Drucker was out for revenge," one of the men stated. "He and his board are crooks; you were in their way."

"That's why he stirred up a couple teachers against you," the lady asserted.

"You stood up for yourself and won your case," said the second teacher. "Your reputation is untarnished."

"Girls High is lucky to have retained you," the lady added. "What other principal would pay half a year's salary for a greenhouse? Who else thought of starting a botanical garden? Who else financed things out of his own pocket? Our school benefits from your generosity."

"Other schools are studying your methods and innovations, sir. Girls' High has become a shining example under your principalship," the first teacher declared.

"When the new board takes over, it may find shortages in the treasury," the second teacher asserted.

Elisha felt better. "Thank you for your show of confidence." He added a little joke to put his friends at ease. Only Nellie knew he was still hurting. She knelt beside him, her face close.

"Even God cannot make it right by everybody, dear. Even our Lord was falsely accused."

He stroked the silky curls that had turned to silver. "I asked Jesus to help me forgive Drucker. I cannot seem to do it by myself, Nellie."

She nodded. "For everything that happens to us there is a reason, dear. Perhaps God used Drucker to tell you something."

"Perhaps He wants me to leave the city, Nellie."

"Leave the city?" Her eyes opened wide.

"I found the most wonderful place on the heights above the hamlet of Ben Lomond. Perhaps we can build a cabin and live there."

She looked askance. "You mean forever? What about the girls?"

"We'll stay in the city until our children have homes of their own." He winked at the lovebirds. "It seems that Myrtle and Charles are about to set a wedding date."

"What about Alice?"

Alice was just coming up the staircase. "Daddy, you're back!" she called out and rushed at him, flinging her arms around his neck. "I always worry about you when you go off by yourself. I'm afraid a grizzly bear or a mountain lion will get you."

Nellie returned to her wicker chair. "Your dad isn't afraid of wild animals, Alice. He's wondering when you're going to get married."

Elisha gasped. It wasn't like Nellie to be so blunt. Alice had played the piano at weddings, but not once had she brought home a suitor.

"We're not rushing you, Alice," Elisha spoke gently. "You can take your time."

Alice looked distraught. "Daddy, I'll never leave you."

He laughed. "You will when the right man comes along!"

"No, Daddy, the young men I meet can't hold a candle to you. They're selfish softies. How can I respect a boy who was pampered by his parents and expects his wife to wait on him?" Alice ran off, crying.

Nellie stopped Elisha from running after her. "Our Alice will remain single, dear. She will play the piano and cheer us in our old age. She'll be a joy to have around."

"But Nellie, a girl must get married."

"No, dear. A girl can be single and happy too."

Six years passed. The moving van was expected at Elisha's house this midsummer morning of 1904. There wasn't much to move. Fred, Joe, and Myrtle, married and settled in homes away from the city, had hauled away objects they liked. Crated items and furniture stood ready for pickup. Elisha riffled through an open box beside the garbage bin and tossed out old magazines. The box had been stored on the "hurricane deck," a stair landing Nellie had named. She and Alice busied themselves on the balcony.

Among the magazines, Elisha found a scrapbook containing published items of speeches he had given at schools and churches, wedding announcements, and parties given for family and camping companions. A large newspaper page wedged itself between the scrapbook's pages. When Elisha unfolded it, a picture of himself stared back at him, surrounded by the smaller pictures of eight prominent teachers. Dated March 5, 1899, the page from the San Francisco *Call* was headlined "Struggles of the Teachers to Get Their Salaries." He read snatches:

The teachers of San Francisco are having a winter of struggle and turmoil, of war and famine. The winter of 1899-1890 will be historic in the annals of the San Francisco schools. . . . The trouble has been caused by the . . . old board, . . . for upon nearing the end of its reckless extravagance and finding a vast shortage about to be disclosed . . . teachers are desperate . . . blame the guilty parties. . . . 'Dishonesty, recklessness, and extravagance,' this is how teachers talk about the late board. There is another meeting at Girls' High. Principal Elisha Brooks has a plan . . . is fighting for the teachers.

He folded the page and returned it to the scrapbook. Scoundrels had blemished his image. At only 63 of age, he was throwing away a lifetime position. He loved Girls' High School, its teachers, and pupils.

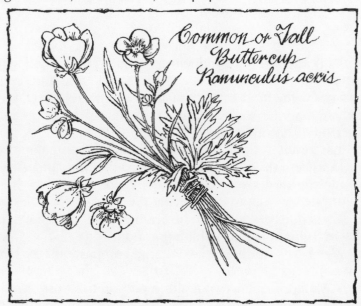

Common or Tall
Buttercup
Ranunculus acris

His chest tightened. Since Drucker's attack, he had endured a feeling of impending doom. He must leave this city, he knew. God had given him a warning he must not ignore. The money shortage caused by the crooked board had forced him get a loan from his brother, Jay, now a merchant in Santa Rosa. Bills for the place at Ben Lomond demanded payment. Where had his salary gone? he wondered. Had he spent it well? Had he been too generous? He had helped support his aging, remarried father. He had given to the church, invested in Girls' High, helped people in need.

Nellie interrupted Elisha's thoughts. "Our children grew up in this house," she sobbed. "Remember when the four youngsters and Jay all had the measles together?"

"You were a wonderful nurse," Elisha praised her. "Now why these tears?"

She sniffled and avoided his question. "I was lucky I didn't get sick myself. I think I had the measles on Nantucket."

"I had the measles in Iowa," Elisha recalled. "There was snow outside and all children in the wagon train got sick."

"We had such good times in this house, Elisha, remember?"

"Yes, Nellie, and we'll create new memories. You'll see!"

"What about our children and grandchildren?"

"They can come and visit anytime."

The moving van rolled to a halt in front and draft horses snorted. Two husky men jumped off and began loading the wagon.

Nellie paled. "I'm not leaving, Elisha!"

He kissed her damp cheek. "Remember Lot's wife, Nellie? It's time to leave this wicked city."

⁂

The flagpole provided a glorious view this Sunday, May

11, 1930. The sun dipped toward the mountains, soon to leave the cloudless sky. Elisha thought all of nature was smiling in gladness. He had climbed the flagpole, as he had done every day since his retirement in 1904. He chuckled to himself. Some people walked a dog because they enjoyed walking. He climbed the flagpole because he enjoyed the view.

His flagpole commanded a sweeping view, situated as it was on a knoll on the brink of a plateau that dipped into the San Lorenzo Valley. The valley stretched several hundred feet below. To the east ranged miles of mountains. Across the valley shimmered white sand dunes, reminders of ocean beaches that had shifted with the upheavals of time. Acres of apple trees he had planted clambered over a hill-side. While pruning, harvesting, crating, and shipping his apples, he had taught local settlers how to make a living.

His house, workshop, fruit packing shed, barn, and camping places for family and friends, extended far beyond his perch. Fruit trees yielded nectarines, plums, oranges, lemons, and other tasty fruit at the proper season. Berry bushes supplied the kitchen with sweet pie fillings. Nellie's rose garden, containing more than a hundred varieties of roses, splashed color and spilled heady perfumes into the air. Paths led to cool ferns in the botanical garden. Rhododendrons and camellias, now past their bloom, had made a magnificent show. Benches invited the visitor to sit, smell, and look. Elisha smiled. Nellie's vegetable garden and his fruit trees provided food year around for themselves and city visitors.

As he unsnapped the flag and draped it over his arm, unbidden thoughts surfaced. Since his arrival at Ben Lomond, he had enjoyed a busy retirement. The passing years had been like weeks of camping in the redwoods. He had taught people of this old mill town how to take pride in their pristine surroundings. His improvement club had given Ben Lomond a community center, a library, and a

124

park. The locals had thanked him with a loving cup and named the library and park after him.

But had he made the best use of his time? he asked himself. *Would Mother be proud of him? Would God approve?*

He had missed the 1906 earthquake, that leveled Girls' High School and ruined their old home in San Francisco.

"God works in wonderful ways," Elisha spoke aloud. "God used Drucker to warn me and get us out in time." He slid down the pole, feeling like a youngster despite his 89 years. Inside the house, he put the flag away.

Nellie called from the kitchen. "Dinner will be ready soon, dear."

"No hurry, Nell."

In the wood-paneled living room, Elisha reached for his reading glasses and opened the large Bible. His wing chair provided welcome comfort. He opened the Bible and read, lips moving silently.

Elisha's chin dropped on his chest, the reading glasses slid down his nose, the book fell to the floor with a thump. Nellie came in from the kitchen. She bent over Elisha and felt for his pulse. He was resting peacefully in death.

Epilogue

❧

In 1850, George Washington Brooks "crossed the plains" to California in search of health, as well as gold. Two years later he sent a letter to his wife, asking her to join him in California. On April 28, 1852, Eliza Ann Scholfield Brooks and her six children set out from their cabin home in St. Joseph County, Michigan, on a 2,800-mile journey in a canvas covered wagon, drawn by four yoke of oxen.

The *Vienna Brooks Saga* has been their story. *California Journey* tells Elisha's story, but what became of Eliza Brooks' other children—Elijah, Justus, Orion, Elmont, Jay, and Joseph? What about Vienna's baby boy? and her husband, John Zumwalt?

Elijah. I have searched diligently for clues shedding light on Elijah's career and adult life. Ever since the night when they had barely escaped being "shanghaied" at the San Francisco waterfront on their journey to Healdsburg, Elijah was terrified of entering that city. Evidently, the twins' pathways separated when Elisha moved to San Francisco.

Sometime during his stay in San Francisco, Elisha and some of his friends made an excursion to Yosemite Valley. He was dressed casually, like a teamster, as they descended into the valley. There they met seven men—one of whom was Elijah! Elisha says, "He could not dodge me, nor I him, though we both would gladly have done so. And the hardest task he ever performed was to introduce his vagabond brother to his dude companions!"

On another outing, Elisha was mistaken for his brother. The incident prompted him to state, "I never felt so flattered in my life, for he [Elijah] is a dapper young man."

On December 6, 1908, when the twins were almost 68 years old, their younger brother, Jay, wrote to Elisha from Santa Rosa:

I returned . . . from a . . . trip near Bidwell Bar. I saw Elijah while there and think he is not making a living. He and Martha are living both at home and are well at present, but Elijah said he had for several months been unable to do any work. He also said that he expected to lose the place he exists on, as it is mortgaged."

In a reply to a letter from Elisha, Jay wrote again on December 16:

Regarding Elijah, I think he would feel out of place at Ben Lomond [the town where Elisha had retired]*; except possibly for a short time. If we could find, and get him to accept, some position where the work was light, though the pay would be small, it would be the easiest solution to the problem. He used to be a fair hand at rough carpenter work."*

Elijah must have visited Elisha at his brother's retirement home in the redwoods, but he didn't stay. Most likely, Elisha helped to support Elijah until the twin's death in 1923, at the age of 82.

Justus. No mention of the adult Justus turns up anywhere in Elisha's papers, nor is he included in a small photo, taken about 1909, that shows Elisha, Elijah, Orion, and Elmont. However, the editor of a booklet Elisha published in 1922 stated that all brothers were living at that time.

Orion. A letter from Orion, written on letterhead of Heald's School of Mines and Engineering, indicates that Orion went into electrical engineering and taught the subject.

Elmont. *The Illustrated History of Sonoma County, California, 1889* mentions Elmont Brooks as "the senior partner of the dry goods and clothing house of Brooks and Loomis in Santa Rosa." It states that Elmont received his practical business education in a dry goods store and was well adapted by nature and education for mercantile business. He was described as "affable, gentlemanly, and honorable in dealing with customers."

Jay. Jay apparently followed Elmont's example, and became a merchant in Santa Rosa.

Joseph. This youngest California-born brother became a carpenter.

Vienna's son and husband. Elisha is strangely silent about Vienna's son and her husband, John Zumwalt. Perhaps the Zumwalt family fiercely protected the child from the Brookses, perceiving them as a threat. You can imagine what Vienna's son must have meant to John—he'd never give up his only living link to Vienna, or even temporarily allow the child out of his sight.

Eliza Ann Scholfield Brooks and her six children reached California in the fall of 1852, after months of unspeakable hardship. Years later, Elisha would write:

I see under the quiet stars a single tent and hear the peaceful snore of six little children, while the mother watches—I doubt that she ever slept . . .

Erna M. Holyer